Sanitarium Magazine
Issue no. 10

Thank you to all of our contributors, we couldn't have done it without you.

Contents

The Boy Who Got Lost in the Woods by James Barton 7

A Witch in the Graveyard by April Williams 15

Loose by Harry Valentine 23

Nevercore by K.P. Hooker 31

The Road to Big Sur by G.D McFetridge 41

Top 10 48

Group Therapy 51

    Plague Inc. 52

    Zombie Evacuation Race 54

    The Woman In Black 60

Reviews 62

The Dust Storm by Ambrose Stolliker 69

The Reverend Gets Stuck in a Hole by Glenn Rolfe 79

Cast Out by John Dennehy 87

The Dark Side by Lex Sinclair 101

Zombie Apocalypse Now! by Rachel Tsoumbakos 111

Dark Verse 119

    I Must By Joseph Patchem 120

    Letter to an Only Friend By Omar ZahZah 121

On The Record: A Moment With Brian Moreland 123

"Where The Horror Happens" with Angeline Trevena 133

ISSUE TEN

I want to take a moment and talk about milestones. In the world of fiction and in particular horror it is always importent to take stock every once in a while and check against your prevoius goals. This could be word count on a WIP, a sales target on published work or it could be a birthday.

We are lucky enough to be in a world where there are such milestones to celebrate. In our Group Therapy session, we are celebrating the 25th year of the West End smash "The Woman in Black", we are also at the end of Rachel Tsoumbakos's Zombie Apocalypse now! ten part saga and we thank her for sharing it with us.

We ourselves are closing in on a milestone - 100 featured stories & dark verse. Who would have thought in just 11 issues we would be at that number? So thank you to all of our readers and contrubutors. Here's to another 100 in the coming issues.

And well done to all those writers who were nominated and to the winners of the Stokers this year.

Welcome to the Sanitarium.

Barry Skelhorn

The Boy Who Got Lost in the Woods

James Barton

Physician: Dr. Roundtree
8245-AVD12

Long ago, in a cottage under the long shadow of the woods, a baby boy entered the light of the world. Mama said he will grow up to be a kind person who would plant magic and happiness in the hearts of all. No, said Papa with hard slap to the table. His son will grow up to be strong, a stonemason like his father. He will be named Stephen after his father and his father's father and his father before him. And Stephen will grow into a mighty man that all men in the kingdom will fear.

Many nights passed as Mama would rock baby Stephen, cooing him to sleep with songs from her childhood. And sometimes as wolves in the distance moaned at the orange moon raging over the night sky, she would notice her baby's gaze turn toward the window and into the darkness of woods beyond.

Stephen grew up into a tow-haired young boy who would sit in Mama's lap while she sewed garments for the king's court and waited for Papa to come home.

"What's in the woods, Mama?"

"Only evil things live in the woods. The darkness has teeth." Mama shook her finger at him. "You must never go there. Little boys don't go into the woods."

"Does Papa live in the woods?"

Mama's eyes were shadowed in sadness as she glanced toward the front door. "Your father is away building beautiful houses for great men of the kingdom. He sends home his gold coins because he loves us so much. You should be very proud of him."

Stephen tilted his head at Mama. "But does no one go into the woods?"

"Only boys who don't love their mother. Come here, Stephen."

Mama pulled a length of red fabric from a roll and dangled it against him.

"Are you making me clothes, Mama?"

"Not for you, sweetie. But you're as tall as Princess Aria. Can you be Mama's little helper?"

Stephen smiled as he nodded his head. "I'm a big boy. As tall as a real princess."

He thought of the beautiful Princess Aria who everyone loved as she strolled through the palace in the beautiful clothes that Mama made. How wonderful to be like her!

Weeks went by as Mama worked on the dress. He would help her with the measurements as she snipped and sewed long into the night under the soft flicker of candlelight. The dress was beautiful with inlaid pearls sewn into the shiny red and gold material. Surely, everyone in the kingdom would love Aria in her new dress. Mama held the dress open as Stephen stepped into it. The dress made a funny crinkles sounds like the snickers of little elves. "Do I look beautiful, Mama? Just like Princess Aria?" The bottom of the dress poofed open like a spring blossom as he twirling in circles.

Mama pinned the dress as Stephen smiled happily at himself in the mirror. He felt tingly as goose bumps tickled his bare shoulders. He tried to imagine his hair longer like Princess Aria. Would everyone now love him just like the princess?

Stephen turned as the door opened. "Papa, Papa, don't I look beautiful?"

Papa's face looked as red as the dress as he stared at Mama. "You put my son in a dress?"

Papa slapped her with the back of his hand. Mama's head made a dull thump as it hit the stone floor. "You do this to my son!" Mama whimpered as Papa kicked her with muddy black boots.

"Get that thing off!" Papa's breath smelled funny as he yanked at the strap.

"Papa, papa, please you're tearing Princess Aria's pretty dress. I was just helping Mama." But the now-tattered dress spilled into a sad little puddle around his feet. Stephen, shivering, covered his nakedness from Papa's angry stare.

Mama whimpered as Papa dragged her into the bedroom, leaving a trail of red like a deer stuck with a hunter's arrow. Stephen went to the window as the door slammed shut. He stared out, trying hard not to hear the sounds on the other side of the door. Papa was growling like a bear while Mama just cried. Stephen could not see past the darkness of the woods. Did the things who lived there fight each other? Was the Papa wolf mean to the Mama wolf? Stephen heard the sounds change on the other side of door as the bed starting croaking like an old witch. Mama was still moaning but it was now different somehow. And it made Stephen feel even funnier inside as he held himself between his legs. He peered back at the window, raising his eyes toward the milky moon high overhead. Mama said boys don't go into the woods. But he wasn't like other boys.

Papa stole Mama's smile, and she stopped sewing. He quickly learned most of Mama's chores while she tried to free the hurt stuck inside her head. But Stephen wasn't sad. He fixed the torn dress using Mama's thread and needle and kept it hidden under his mattress. At night Stephen would take out the dress as the wolves sang to him from the woods. It felt cool as he pressed it against his bare skin, imagining he was the beautiful princess who everyone would love.

And it came to pass a short time later, a new family moved in at the farm around the bend of the river. He met Little Red one day while he fetched water for Mama. Her real name was Annalise but her grandma called her Little Red because her hair was kissed by the sunset. Just like him, Red had no brothers or sisters to play with. Stephen didn't know any girls, but Red seemed nice just the same as they played in her barn and took walks together. Sometimes they would venture close enough to the woods to see shadows moving inside. But Red pulled him back, saying her grandma told her that danger lived in the woods.

One day inside her barn, Little Red suggested they play knights and ladies. Stephen said he could play Princess Aria. And Red just laughed, saying he was a boy.

But Stephen said he was not like other boys. When he pulled out his dress he was afraid she would laugh.

Her hands caressed the soft material. "This is yours? You really wear it?"

"Close your eyes." When he told her it was safe to open her eyes, Red just stared at him silently as she walked toward him, stepping around his pile of his clothes lying on the straw. Sparks danced inside her cat-green eyes as she leaned her head close to him.

There was a wet smack as she pressed her lips on his.

"Hey!" He wiped his mouth with the back of his hand.

"You're like the sister I never had." She giggled until he forgot he was mad and started laughing with her.

After they played for a while, Red said she wanted to be Princess Aria now. Stephen removed his dress, holding it carefully in front of him so she couldn't see his nakedness. But Red didn't make him close his eyes as she, with a shy smile, removed all her clothes. Feeling his cheeks burning, he slowly lowered his dress. Red didn't look much like Mama. She was slim and short with smooth pink skin, glowing in the sparkle of the sunlight. Stephen pressed his thighs together as he saw her wide eyes wandering downward.

When he told her they both looked like skinned squirrels, she giggled into her hand. They could have been twin sisters.

When she slipped on the dress, pulling back her long red braids over her shoulders, she lifted her chin comically high like the real Princess Aria until they were both snorting with laughter. As he pulled her blue spring dress over his head, he breathed in her earthy scent of wildflowers and straw. He smoothed down her dress against his body as they both studied each other in a spill of sunlight from outside the barn. It was like gazing into a mirror: her dress fit him perfectly as his did on her. She broke the silence with a curtsey, asking him to dance.

"But I don't know how ..." She took his hands in hers and they held each other, sharing their warmth as their feet swept them away to a place of magic where nothing else mattered.

Mama mostly napped the afternoons when Stephen went to see Little Red. And Papa was never home. Walking to Red's house, carrying his dress in a basket, he would sometimes hear voices whisper to him from woods. But he tried his best to ignore them. Only boys who don't love their mother went into the woods.

And a time came a few years later when the dress became too small for him. He let out the seams and sewed in some different material from Mama's sewing box. But the dress looked sad, more like a quilt and not anything that Princess Aria would ever wear. Little Red didn't seem to mind, but she seemed bored of tea parties, sometimes wanting to just kiss. But were sisters supposed to kiss all the time?

Already taller than Mama, he was frightened by the changes he saw in his body. His soft skin turned veiny, and coarse like Papa's. His voice deepened, sounding the low growl of a wild animal. And dark hair, began sprouting everywhere like a thatch of brush in the woods. He pulled and plucked and scraped until he was raw and red so that no one would see what he was becoming. But voices in the woods seemed to know. Sometimes outside his window under the blue gaze of the moon, he would see a flash of yellow eyes staring back, whispering to him to join them.

Red didn't understand why he now had to change in a stall. But he didn't dare let her see what he had become. And one day just after he put on his dress, Red gave him a curious half-moon grin as she unbuttoned hers. Do you want to switch already? he asked. Without a word, she peeled off her clothes. Standing naked under the high relief of shadows from the late afternoon sun, she gave her button nose a playful twitch as she took his hand, pulling him downward with her into the bed of hay. Red looked more like Mama now, with wide hips and curves over her body. Cocooning him in her warmth, she pressed her moist lips on his, drowning him in her bubby wave of intensity. Her bare breasts flattened against his chest as she wrapped her thighs over his knee. Black streamers floated across his vision as she lifted up her head from him.

"Do you ever feel …" Her pink lips lifted upward into a lopsided grin as her hand brushed against his cheek. "…like doing something more than just kiss?" Stephen gasped as he felt her heated fingers creep under his dress. Did she know that he had changed? Would she now be afraid of this wild thing he had become?

But she stopped as her hand touched the softness at the junction of his thighs. Confusion bloomed inside her eyes.

"Don't you like me, Stephen? She stroked his softness between her fingers. "Am I not doing it right?"

"Please … don't." His voice was a pained whisper as he gently placed his hand on top of hers through his dress.

"Aren't boys are supposed to like girls?"

"I'm not like the other boys," he said as he rolled her off and shot upward to his feet. She shouted at him but he was already out the door. He ran until his chest was heaving and his breath was ragged in his chest. And he realized now the magic of childhood was now gone. The long summer of play with Little Red, the tea parties, their laughs together, their dances, had passed like the falling of golden and red leaves in the chill of autumn. They could never be sisters again because he had changed. And he could never go home or be with Little Red again. He wasn't like the other boys.

As the sun fell behind the woods and the dark blanket of stars opened its stern orange eye on him, he heard the rustling of movements deeper within. Stephen followed the trail of breathy whispers into the woods. And he was never seen again.

Little Red grew up and married a kindly shoemaker. And together they had a beautiful baby son with chubby cheeks and a bubbly laugh. At night, as Little Red rocked her little one to sleep, she would sometimes turn her eyes to the window toward the crisp blue moon holding back the darkness of the sky. And she would imagine someone whispering her name from somewhere in the woods. At those times she would think of a curious friend from long ago when the summer would never end and where magic still danced in the light of day. He wasn't like the other boys. And during those times Little Red would clutch her baby boy tightly against her breast to keep him warm against the chill of the night.

The End.

A Witch in the Graveyard

April Williams

Physician: Dr. Peterson
8268-WCT29

The gauzy shadow entwines with the penumbrae of trees and tombstones. They blend and morph as he squints at the monitor. The glow of the surrounding city provides questionable light and thick clouds extinguished the moon and stars hours ago. Antiquated security cameras are of debatable help. Brady never knows when they will feel like working. As he peers for discernment between human or ghost, there is movement on camera 3's monitor. Before he can register what he sees, the image jumps to camera 5.

In Brady's ten years as overnight security guard for Eternal Peace Cemetery, he has seen hundreds of thrill-seeking kids. They are the predominant reason for his job. He has also experienced ghosts in moderate numbers. Amorphous countenances that waver and moan. Hover and scream. They appear and disappear from his senses unpredictably; tingling his nerves and chilling his skin. The first few times he witnessed them, terror ripped through him and he nearly peed his pants. Now he accepts them as another aspect of the job. On nights when he doesn't see any ghosts, he feels a bit bored and lonely. The images he is witnessing on the monitors are different. Iciness crawls along his spine and he shudders to release it. He cannot determine if what he is seeing is human or ghost.

"Damn, I suppose I better go check it out." The nervousness he hears in his voice sparks fear.

He grabs his flashlight and switches the safety of his gun to "off".

"A lotta' good a gun will do me if it is a ghost," he mutters.

The yellowish beam of light cuts eerily into the darkness as he heads for the area monitored by camera 3. He is nearly there when a figure seems to float out from behind a ten-foot headstone of an angel. Startle response jolts him for a moment. He regains his composure quickly but can feel his heart thud against his shirt.

He shines the flashlight at the figure's face. Even thought the battery is fully charged, the light flickers. The dimness disfigures the image and casts shadows like clouds racing across the moon. He only sees a wavering part of her smile. The shadowed red lips and gleaming scattered teeth pop goose bumps in his arms. He grips the flashlight tightly with one hand and places the other on the butt of his gun. Even he feels the shameful feebleness in this attempt to show authority.

"It's 3:00 a m. Who are you and why are you here?" he asks in the strongest voice he can find.

"This cemetery doesn't have locked gates and I am causing no harm. Why are you questioning me?"

Her voice is black velvet. Soothing and foreboding. Brady should feel relief that this is a human being. But he doesn't.

As he is about to answer, her shadowed hand plunges down into the darkness. She pulls a mole up by the scruff of its' neck. The little creature shrieks and kicks helplessly in her grasp. Brady guides the flashlight to the mole and gulps. The shadowy woman holds the mole to within inches of her face.

"Be still," she whispers firmly. It quiets at once. Except for the heart beat.

"It is disrespectful to burrow into graves. And since it is also disrespectful to harm living things, I will let you go under a condition. You and your fellow moles must depart from here at once and do not come back."

With that, she gently sets the creature back on the ground. Instantly, countless unseen moles scuttle from their holes. Their little claws tear up tufts of grass as they run like a miniature stampede. A lone night hawk screeches. It dives down and grasps one of the moles in its' hungry talons. It screeches again as it flies off to enjoy the meal. The woman smiles then returns her attention to Brady.

"Now will you answer me, please?" she asks.

Brady realizes his mouth is agape. Even in the dim light, that was the freakiest, creepiest thing he has ever seen a person do. He feels so fascinated that he momentarily forgets where he is and why he is here. Then he closes his mouth, clears his throat and slowly returns to being a security guard.

"Um…I'm questioning you because other than kids, it's rare for anyone to be in the cemetery in the middle of the night…"

The shriek of the now distant night hawk interrupts him. An image of the mole being slashed to shreds flashes in his mind. He involuntarily shivers. She waits patiently.

"…And um…as a security guard, it is my responsibility to keep the premises unharmed."

"That sounds reasonable. And I assure you that I mean no harm."

God, that voice! Brady has schizoid feelings of both wanting to nestle in it and run screaming.

"My name is Sofia. I live a few blocks away from here. As you may have guessed, I am a witch. And I am here to extend invitations"

He does and doesn't want to know. Kind of like driving by an accident.

"Invitations?"

"Yes," she replies crisply. "Shine your flashlight into the basket I am carrying."

He does so with a shaky hand and before he can look at the contents, he notices that the beam of light in now steady. Not even a hint of a flicker. The basket contains a variety of herbs, both fresh and powered. There are candles, oils incense and a few objects that Brady doesn't recognize. Nothing in the basket is even close to traditional paper and envelope invitations. He looks to her in the shadows for explanation.

"I am inviting earth-bound spirits to move on. Certainly you have experienced spirits in your time working here."

This is a statement, not a question. And yet it still demands an answer. Brady shuffles his feet and coughs nervously.

"Of course I have but I still don't understand why you are here."

"There are myriads of spirits who get trapped here on earth, Brady. May I call you Brady?"

He has no idea how she knows his name. But rather that feeling compelled to question her about it, he simply nods.

"Many of them stay close to the remains of the bodies in which they once resided. Some stay here by choice, others just visit periodically but most would love to move on to other realms. Every year a certain number of witches are assigned locations to search for such spirits and give them invitations. I am doing that with the items in this basket. Then on Halloween night, if they so choose, they will be free to go."

A multitude of questions spin in Brady's mind. Yet all his tongue can find to say is, "Halloween is two nights away."

"Yes!"

Excitement dances in her single word.

"I might call in sick that night."

Her spontaneous laughter verges on cackle.

"That might not be a wise choice, Brady."

Before he can ask why, he feels a small patch of grass and earth shift below him. He shines the light down and gasps. Tree roots crawl up from under the ground. They twist around his ankle and climb his leg like slithering snakes. He tries to run backwards and is pulled down by the tension. Sounds he didn't know he is capable of lurch from his mouth. Sofia quickly reaches into her basket and extracts a packet of iron filings. She gently scatters them onto the desperate tree roots while chanting softly in Enochian tongue. They hesitate for a moment then slowly slide off Brady's leg and slink back into the earth. Brady scrambles clumsily to his feet and fights to catch his breath. The flashlight splays on the ground where he fell, shining light on a gargoyle tombstone that he didn't know was there. Sofia picks it up and gently hands it to him.

"Your fear will be gone in moments," she says softly. "The spirits here know and trust you. You have been their protector for many years. This poor soul was just a bit over eager. It meant you no harm. Please work your shift on Halloween. They need you and you may even be granted a surprise."

With that, she walks into the shadows. The beam of light can't even find her. Brady gulps hard and runs back to the security building. He slams the door and turns the deadbolt with more pressure than is necessary. A false sense of security. He quickly peruses the monitors. There is no sight of her. He feels a momentary relief. Then each of the five screens begin to fill with ghosts. He has never seen this many. Ever. He feels overwhelmed and covers his mouth with his hand to stop the screams.

The next night at work, Brady deliberately looks for Sofia. Although he doesn't really want to see her again, he has many questions. He nervously figures that she is the only one who knows the answers. After staring at the monitors for over three hours, his eyes burn. He saw tombstones, tree shadows and ghosts. But no Sofia. He decides to take to take the golf cart out of the caretaker's shed. More area can be covered quickly and he won't have to put to his feet on the ground. He shudders at the thought of the creepy tree roots turning him into a trellis.

As he drives along the paths then around the gravestones and trees, he begins to notice a variety of fragrances. Cinnamon, fresh cut grass and sandalwood are purely intoxicating. But others are disgusting. He smells skunk and rotten eggs. They are so strong; he coughs and pulls his shirt up over his mouth and nose. As the aromas blend and change without pattern or warning, Brady continues his search for Sofia. She is nowhere to be found. After more than an hour of this fruitless endeavor, he decides to go back to the shed. As he rounds the mausoleum, a huge ghost, the color of dirty steam, jumps up in front of him. Before Brady can even think, the spirit moans, laughs and passes right through him. Brady shrieks and wonders frantically how many moments he has left to live.

He stops and sits statue still. A cool, refreshing feeling permeates his entire being. But even though this feels pleasant, he is still terrified. He guns the cart to its' maximum speed of 20 mph and returns to the shed. For the remainder of his shift, he stays locked in his office and watches television. Infomercials suck but they are better than watching the images on the monitors. He no longer cares if she shows up or not.

The next day is Halloween and Brady spends hours obsessing about calling in sick. He finally decides to man up and go to work. He can't let that woman frighten him anymore. After all, he has worked there ten years and nothing serious has happened. How bad could it be?! And although he isn't a big fan of surprises, he doesn't want to take the risk of making anyone or anything angry.

The first hour of his shift is calm, although he is not. He stays locked in his office, vacillating between the monitors and the windows. For the second time this week, he is seeing a record number of ghosts. Some are mesmerizing and beautiful. Almost hypnotic. While others are so hideous, Brady gags.

Then the moaning starts. A low-grade mournful sound in the distance. Then sporadic shrieks pierce the air, like a thousand night hawks. Brady desperately covers his ears. Howls and growls, filled with pain and anger, reverberate through the graveyard. Tree branches begin to creak and crack. Then hundreds of them thunder to the ground. A large oak tree falls just outside Brady's window, narrowly missing the building. He screams and jumps.

Although the sky is cloudless, lightening flashes and thunder crashes. Screeching winds toss marble tombstones like confetti. Bony, nebulous arms, twist and scratch at the air. A cornucopia of colors spark and twinkle, misting the air with a glitter-like substance. The aromas of yesterday return tenfold. Tantalizing scents of fresh baked bread and lilacs in bloom swirl violently with painful odors of sewage and rotting corpses. As the smells infiltrate his office, Brady instinctively lights candles then curls up into a ball, underneath his desk.

The bizarre activity spreads from the cemetery to the surrounding city. Seven church steeples snap from their bases like twigs and crash to the ground. They destroy everything and anyone in their paths. Thirteen inmates incarcerated for murder and rape, die instantly with no harm to anyone around them. Judge's chambers and lawyer's offices burst into flame while their neighbors remain unscathed. Random people are invisibly beaten and emergency vehicles rendered powerless. And diffused throughout the chaos, thousands of people feel mysterious caresses on their cheeks and hug-like sensations around their shoulders.

The cacophony of sound, light and smell escalates to the point where Brady can no longer hear his own screams. But through the din, he can hear the knock on his door. He curls paralyzed, hoping against hope that it will just go away. It doesn't. The knocking becomes furious pounding. Continuous and more thunderous than the noises outside. Feeling totally against his will, he finally crawls out from under the desk and opens the door. Sofia wafts in and like flipping a switch, the air becomes eerily quiet. Not a sound, except his heart beat. The only remnant of the chaos is a rainbow colored glow that slowly fades into the sky.

Brady gulps and closes his eyes. He realizes how severely he is trembling and sits down.

"It's midnight. Those that wanted to, have departed," Sofia says softly.

She then extracts a thermos and two cups from her basket. After she hands him the cup, he chugs it down. He doesn't care what it is or how hot. Until after he drinks it and burns his mouth. He is about to shout out when he notices that the door on the small refrigerator is opening of its' own accord. Watching with wide-eyed fascination, a bottle of water lifts and floats through the air then gently presses itself against his lips for a moment. Then the cap twists off and cool water is placed on his lips and tongue. The pain stops immediately.

"What the hell?!" These are the only words Brady's brain can muster.

Sofia smiles brightly and she is beautiful. Brady feels very confused. As he is trying to gather his wits, a bluish-white spirit makes itself visible. It pats Brady on the head and begins to tidy the office. In all Brady's years, he has never seen a spirit in the office. He feels overwhelmed with fear and awe.

Sofia finally speaks, still smiling.

"I was right. You did get a surprise. You now have a personal spirit. And a helpful one at that. This is absolutely wonderful!"

"Huh," is all he can think to say.

They sit in silence for a long time, drinking their tea and watching the spirit. Brady's fears begin to calm and he actually starts to like this spirit. He also loses his anxiety toward Sofia and decides that even though she is still a bit creepy, she really is a good witch. Of all the questions he had earlier, now he has only one.

"Are they really gone now?"

"Yes. Very few chose to stay behind and as you can see with your new friend, they are benevolent."

"Oh, thank God!" Brady sighs.

"But you need to remember, Brady, fresh bodies are buried in this cemetery on a nearly daily basis…"

Brady shivers and the spirit laughs.

The End.

Loose

Harry Valentine

Physician: Dr. Edgar
9328-SJE41

It didn't happen all at once.

Sean was sitting in his car driving hungover and maybe a little drunk and he felt a twitching under his arm that, for some reason, didn't alarm him. That might have been strange – that an uncontrolled muscle spasm didn't alarm him, but he had other things to think about than the jumping ball of muscle halfway down his ribs.

He was thinking about the night before at the concert when he was trying to dance with Heather but he couldn't do it. His hips wouldn't move the way he wanted them to and his feet were stuck to the ground, partially because of the tacky concrete floor, mostly because he didn't exactly know when or how to move. So he just sort of bobbed with his chest and let his neck snap back and forth. It was not impressive.

Every concert he had ever been to had that moment where he wished he wasn't there, a disconnect between the music and the things he had to do. He had to hold his coat or wait for the next band or pretend to sing along to the new songs he didn't know. The worst though, was when he had to pretend he knew what dancing was, which he very much didn't.

It had never made sense to him. He sang along to songs, he occasionally hopped on his heels or nodded his head in rhythm. But if he put his arm into the air or shuffled his feet he was certain he would look like some kind Seizing Freak. To him, every guy that danced looked like a Seizing Freak. Girls were okay. They could get away with dancing.

This is what Sean was thinking about when he was driving his car hungover and maybe a little drunk, and these were the thoughts that kept him distracted from the thumping muscle under his arm. Within a few minutes, it passed, but he had forgotten it by then.

He pulled into his parents' driveway. Visiting home was weird, and he didn't like it. It was good to see friends, technically, but seeing old friends could be just as awkward as dancing, so he avoided them, which didn't help. He avoided his parents too, and spent most of his time visiting concerts and staring at screens. The television and the laptop were not exhausting, neither was his phone. It passed the time, and whether he liked to admit it or not, that's what he was doing. Passing time.

It was a little different with Heather. She lived in town, but she didn't annoy him. Time with her didn't pass, it flew. He wished she would call; he never knew when it was okay to call.

He unbuckled his seatbelt as he slid into the driveway. Car in park, emergency brake on, key turned and out, feet on the driveway, door closed: his moves were practiced, familiar. He reached out and tapped the side of his car.

He was halfway up the driveway before he realized that he hadn't meant to do that – to reach out and tap his fingers against the door of his car. Weird. He turned around and picked up the newspaper. Dad liked it when he brought in the newspaper.

He came into the house and his knees were ambushed by the dog. Her name was Tallypo. Half crouched; he ran his fingers in her fur as she followed him down the staircase to the guestroom that used be his bedroom, and onto the bed.

He slept until the late afternoon. It was already getting dark and Mom was predictably furious with Dad but masking it by jumping into the ongoing fight about his lack of drive. She wanted him to take out the trash to unload the dishwasher to walk the dog to vacuum the house. He had built up the idea of vacation in his mind; she had built up the idea of having her boy back. He stumbled out of the bed and called up that he had taken the paper in already and he would be up in a second.

He peed for what felt like thirty minutes, but what might have actually been two, and then started. He sort of turned his brain off as he brushed his teeth, and didn't turn it on until he had taken out the trash and taken in the recycling and eaten some breakfast and unloaded the dishwasher and taken the ornaments off of the Christmas tree. At some point while unscrewing the base, his eyes fell out of focus and he didn't bother to adjust them. This is how he was when he hauled the tree out of the house.

He knew it was shedding but he didn't care. He walked out of the door and saw that it was almost full dark outside. Purple-gray. He hauled the tree out past the porch and into the backyard. His feet were aiming towards a fence. He would throw the tree over that fence and all of his problems could be solved. He would just wash the sap off of his hands, open up his laptop and finally relax.

He set the tree down just before the fence, yanked off a short branch near the top and jammed it in his mouth. It tasted sweet and earthy. It was strange that he hadn't meant to do that. He spit the dry, tacky twig out onto the ground and quickly walked in out of the cold.

Mom was waiting just inside, prepared to tell him he had done something wrong, but he didn't hear her. He told her he was going to the bathroom. That usually bought him some time.

He wanted to brush the pine needles off of his lips but never got to it.

He made it two steps down before he collapsed completely. His eyes were open the whole time, and he saw the hallway slipping away and the hard wood stairs rolling over him. He landed on his neck with a quiet crack.

He woke up a week later in the hospital and no one would tell him what was happening. The problem was, he couldn't ask. Whenever he tried to his lips would clamp shut. Instead, he said things he didn't mean to. It was an altogether alien experience to feel his lips flap, his tongue wiggle, and his throat close up, all to make words he hadn't thought of. Against his will, he apologized to Mom for not being a good son. He felt his cheeks quiver and his eyes hurt as Dad cried. It took him some time to understand why his breathing was labored, why his throat hurt, why the snot was running into his mouth. He was crying.

The hug he got from Dad felt nice. The ones from Mom too. He hadn't had those in a while.

He thought that maybe it had something to do with the fall. He had broken something in his neck, he knew that much. Was there such a thing as reverse-paralysis? He could still move; he just wasn't in control of it. So what was?

He had been awake for two days before he started to think about the twitch that morning, the tap on the car, the taste of pine in his mouth. The collapse on the stairs. Doctors told him he had slipped, but Sean remembered a kick he didn't start.

He was home sooner than anyone expected. They said he was recovering fast, but he knew he was no better. He was worse. He wasn't the one getting better, shuffling along the hospital hallways, gripping an IV stand. He was helpless. He had no control over his body, over his mouth. Over the things he did. He was helpless, but something in his body was helping itself.

Tallypo didn't want to play. The first week he came back, she barked at him constantly. He could hear her bark get raspier as that first week dragged on. When he used to live at home, she would lie next to him if he wasn't feeling well. But when he came back from the hospital, she barked so much that Mom and Dad locked her in the laundry room. She still growled and whimpered, but by the end of each night, she had worn herself out.

She never got used to him.

Without meaning to say it, he said that he wasn't ready to go back to school. Without meaning it, he was very convincing and his parents understood. He was stuck in his body. And they were stuck at home.

One night Sean's eyes were opened and he sat up in bed. Back straight, lips loose, head cocked at an angle as if listening to something, feet on the floor. Whatever moved him was getting slicker, more polished, almost familiar.

The two of them, he and his body, moved down the hallway. He could feel the cold wood on his feet and had the instinct to walk on his toes but that of course didn't lead to anything. He wished he could get socks.

His breath was ragged, which was unusual. Ever since he came home his breath had been calm, cool, under control. He could feel the hand tremble as it gripped the cold doorknob to his parents' bedroom. For the first time since the hospital, he felt in synch with his body. They were both terrified.

The forehead rested on the door, and after a sharp intake of breath, the door was open and they were inside.

Sean tried not to watch as his eyes fixed on Mom's face. He tried to be quiet as his body snuck around the side of the bed, but his body was quiet enough. His eyes locked onto Dad's neck. Whatever he was now was checking for something.

He felt himself crouch, as if to get a closer look. His knees made a sharp pop as he settled in. His body tightened at the sound, and Sean realized that maybe it wasn't fear he had felt. Maybe, it was anticipation.

Sean realized he was looking at himself. His head had turned swiftly and he was facing a mirror. He stayed that way for some time. Unmoving. Watching his familiar face grow more foreign, more unusual with each passing moment. Sean was relieved when his body arose and crept towards the door.

He tried to fight what happened next – the final turn of the head and flick of the eyes that revealed Mom's heartbeat pulsing in her neck – but there was no fighting. He couldn't will his eyes forward. His feet were quiet as he slipped out of the room and down the stairs and into the laundry room and Tallypo only got one bark out before she was silenced and after a while he stopped feeling her heartbeat under the fingertips.

Sean knew he had to do something, but that was exactly the problem. He daydreamed of being a character in a movie, of how he would train his mind to overpower his body. He would focus inward and overpower whatever force was controlling him. But he couldn't flick an eyelid. When his eyes closed, it got dark. When his body read something, he had to read it too. Where his body went, he went, and there was no deep recess of his mind to build up a defense. In the battle between mind over matter, matter had won. He was happy to go back to bed.

Tallypo was a very old dog and no one thought she had been strangled.

His body pretended to be very sad for several days, but Sean of course was not convinced. He thought of the way the way he had been forced to stare at Dad's throat. Nothing suspicious happened for the next several days. If he could have screamed, he would have told Mom how strange it was that he was acting so normal. That he was reading everyday and exercising and not screaming.

Heather called. She hadn't heard about the accident, which frustrated Sean in a way he didn't expect, but his body didn't tell her. Before, a call from Heather meant warmth. It meant happiness; it meant an excited feeling from his chest to his toes. Now, all he could feel was a coldness. He knew his grip on the phone was tightening, and it made him sick. She had called to tell him about a concert.

Sean's body agreed to meet her there.

Sean's parents were nervous about his first day driving, about his first day out of the house, but he assured them he would be fine. He wished he wasn't doing that. He wanted to tell them to tie him to a chair, to call the police, to call the hospital, to cover their throats. But nothing would come out of his mouth, of course, except reassurance.

Sean's body was a very cautious driver, but when he got to the concert, it was more graceful than it had been when Sean was in charge of it. When it met Heather, it was more charming. And when it danced to the music, it was like nothing he had ever felt. There was an electricity pumping through his body, a quickness in his step, a boldness in his fingers. He touched Heather confidently, pulling her close and letting her go at what Sean never would have guessed would be the right times. Sean wanted to watch her, but his eyes were glued to the band. His body was not concerned with the tacky floor or the social rules of the dance floor. His body wanted touch and pursued it. His body heard music and let it flow through him.

Sean wanted some water so he went to order a drink. He had taken three steps before he realized that they were intentional. More than that, the feet were following his intention. He had chosen to do something, and it had happened. He tried to lick his lips, and he did. He chose to clench his hands, and as he lifted his arms high, he could see himself forming fists.

And there was a moment where he thought, very clearly, that he had just gotten off of a roller coaster. He watched the people dancing around him and he stood still, shaking his fists and licking his lips. He wondered if he could ride it again, just for a minute, just until he left the club.

But then he was running. And even though he hadn't decided to, he knew that it really was him running because he had to get away from here because these people weren't safe and it wasn't fair and he forced himself to suck in the cold fresh air when he burst from the doors and as he rounded a corner into a brick alley he heard her voice behind him.

"Sean," Heather said.

He clenched his fists tighter and hung his head but she tapped his shoulder, and when his head turned to look at her, he couldn't be sure if his body was in control or if he was in control. He had wanted to turn, and he had turned.

Sean looked into Heather's eyes and saw her staring into his. She was close, and she seemed to be looking past him, through his eyes, into something deeper. He wanted to kiss her. He knew he did, but he didn't know how.

He knew if he tried to kiss her he could but he was too afraid so by some instinct he forced himself to relax so his body took over and leaned in gently and kissed Heather on the mouth and Sean wanted that control back but he couldn't have it now it was too late he knew he had given it up and his body yanked Heather closer to him and he could feel her struggling but his body didn't let up and mashed his mouth against hers until she relaxed and then his body let hers go.

She took a step back, and so did he.

Without even realizing it, she smiled.

Without meaning to, his eyes flicked to her neck.

Sean watched his hands rise. No longer responding, they hung like rags as they moved towards her.

All he could do was try to close his eyes.

The End.

Nevercore

K.P Hooker

Physician: Dr. Lotherton
8715-AED19

"Okay, first things first, I have to look at porn." "Don't! My parents check the history!" "Relaaaax," he said, "I'm just kidding."

Of course Eli was kidding. He once called Maddy the "quintessential little sister". It pained her twice knowing that he thought of her as a sister and his use of the word "quintessential" making him all the more appealing. Though she tried to hide her natural uptight tendencies under a rebel guise, they slipped out in moments of panic, and panic was never in short supply.

Maddy and Eli were hip to hip in one desk chair in her parent's study, both with damp hair from recently rinsing out dye. Pink this time. She wasn't allowed to have boys over in an empty house, but was prepared to claim that they were doing homework should they come home sooner than expected. And it wouldn't be a lie if she could trick Eli into something like homework.

"Hey, divide 156 by 12."

"13. Why?"

"Fun." She felt 70% less guilty.

"Help me find a skull to buy. I want one for the ol' terrarium," Eli said. He searched the word "skull" in google images.

"What's a terrarium?" she asked.

"It's like an aquarium, but without water and you decorate it with dirt and plants and skulls and put your lizard in it. Sparky's gonna love it," he said.

Maddy pictured a rectangle of desert lifted out of the ground and implanted in Eli's room. She knew he wanted to go camping in Joshua tree and that was as close as he could get at the moment.

"Now where should I search for a skull to buy?" Eli asked.

Maddy sidled her hands up to his on the keyboard brushing the side of her pinky up his on the way. She typed the address for a crafty website where anyone could sell their artisanal goods, even shitty ones. The homepage filled out with ruffled aprons, found objects, leather jewelry, and an empty, rusty soup can mounted on a trophy base.

Eli searched "real skull". The results were pleasing. All down the page there were skulls from raccoons, pigs, foxes, squirrels. The more expensive items were entire animals whose bones were each lovingly removed from a carcass, cleaned, preserved, and hitched back together like a dinosaur in a museum.

Maddy imagined skinning a squirrel and cutting its insides apart. It seemed like something only a sick person would do, but someone had to do it. Probably everyone used to do it a long time ago, she thought. And yet if she wanted to learn how, her parents would probably put her back in therapy. It's only bad if you're doing it for fun and not even using the all the animal parts, she thought. Using a skull as decoration was actually very prudent.

"I wonder if it's legal to sell a human skull. Because then it's like, how did you get it? How did you acquire a human skull?" Maddy said.

"That would be awesome."

"That would be creepy. Like they might haunt you." Eli checked the box that limited the items to ones in and around Portland, Oregon. The results were narrowed down and overwhelmingly from one seller. He clicked on a twenty-dollar raccoon skull to view more photos.

"Click on the picture with the guy in it," Maddy said.

The image filled out the screen. A shirtless man held up the skull in the foreground for the camera, but his face was obscured and his body a blur. Apparently a taxidermy enthusiast, he wore an animal skin mask. It was unclear what animal the face had come from, but it was laced around his head and only covered the upper half. The hand that supported the skull appeared yellowed on the dry areas and rough with dirty work. All over his exposed body, he had wiry black hair, even on his fingers.

"This guy is…" Eli didn't know.

"A serial killer! What other items does he have?" Maddy asked.

Eli clicked on the seller's name: Nevercore.

"Kind of an awesome name," he said, "Sounds like a good band name."

Nevercore's shop was a mess of preserved animal bits and pieces. It was mostly skulls, bones, feet, and fur. Some of the fur was an animal's face ready to be a mask with leather strings to tie it back just like the one Nevercore was wearing in any pictures he appeared in. *Masquerade dress-up animal fur taxidermy mask*, the search terms read. The masks did not live up to the glamor of a masquerade ball with their jagged edges and misshapen eye holes. The one fully stuffed animal sold by Nevercore was a horrorstruck squirrel, doomed to have bulging eyes forever with a small crust of glue in each tear duct.

"This person is crazy. Do you think he hunts and eats the animals?" Maddy asked.

"Maybe. Some people eat squirrel, that doesn't make him crazy," Eli answered.

"Agreed. In fact, I have a right mind to try squirrel sometime. But these pictures are kind of messed up right?"

"They're weird. I don't know, maybe they're art. Maybe this guy is really cool."

"There's something disturbing about it, though. Masks are disturbing. The mask combined with the animal parts and the shirtlessness… the question is, is he being weird on purpose?"

"Well, weird of not, he's in Gresham, so I'm going to ask if we can come buy the raccoon skull in person to save on shipping."

"We? No. Neither of us are going out there."

Eli and Maddy turned to each other, their noses inches apart.

"Please, Maddy? I need a ride!" "I'll just pay the shipping, geeze."

"But it'll be an adventure. Aren't you curious about the kind of person that would dedicate their life to sprucing up roadkill? We can write about it on our applications to art school. Plus we can browse all the cool stuff he has. And if you feel weird, you can wait in the car. Please?"

Eli wrapped an arm around Maddy's waist and let his head fall on her shoulder. It wasn't like him to grovel.

Maddy conceded, "Will you buy me a ginger beer before we go?"

Eli smiled and clicked on a link that read "Contact Nevercore".

***

The road through Gresham saw the houses grow further apart from one another. They passed U-Pick berry farms that were closed in the grey winter weather. Eli turned up the music and mocked Maddy's serious face.

"You're like, leaning forward while you drive. Like a little old lady. And why did you take your boot off?"

"I can't drive with that boot on. It's too stiff," Maddy said, eyes rarely blinking. Specs of rain dusted the windshield; the drops so tiny that the wipers skidded across them. Her phone's map dictated the final turn on a road that technically dead-ended, but continued on dirt. Nevercore's little house sat just before the dirt road began.

The lawn was kept simply. It was cut and clean, but without bushes or winter-empty flower pots. Two rocking chairs swayed on the front porch out of synch as if two invisible people were rocking at different paces.

Maddy stuffed her leg back into her rain boot.

"Do you think he'll answer the door wearing one of those masks?" Eli asked.

"God, I hope not," Maddy took a final swig of ginger beer, "OK, let's get you a skull."

While they approached the house a curtain parted briefly and the front door opened.

"You Eli?" the man asked.

Maddy was relieved at his sight. He was a greying man who wore khakis and a flannel shirt tucked in. His beer gut only served to make him look folksy. She forgot everything that had made him seem creepy in the first place.

"Raccoon skull, right?"

"Yessir," Eli said.

"Well, raccoon skulls, I have many, but I have a lot more stuff too. Care to come in and take a look?"

"We'd rather see them here on the front porch," Maddy said. "I could bring out a few things, but there's too much to bring it all," the man said.

"Let's just go in, Mad," Eli said, "I want to see everything."

"Sure," Maddy said. It had slipped out automatically. Her subconscious was telling the world that she was no wet blanket. As she walked across the threshold she realized she was risking her life to seem easygoing and for a raccoon skull that she could have paid $5 to have delivered to her doorstep. The police would have to tell her parents that, yes, she had been imprisoned in a cellar and dismembered by a crazed taxidermist, but at least she was polite enough to come in when invited.

Though kept tidy, the house had not had any updates in decades and smelled of a litter box someplace. Maddy saw an ash tray with a mountain of butts ready to tumble apart and she couldn't remember ever having seen someone smoke indoors in her life. She planted her feet just inside the front door and watched as Eli followed the man without question.

"Excuse me. Where are you taking us?" she asked.

"The workshop's down in the basement," he answered.

"You can stay up here if you want," Eli offered, but Maddy couldn't bear the thought of Eli going alone or the fact that she would have to make a choice between running away and rescuing him should he scream.

"No, I'll come." Maddy joined them, trailing behind. She glanced at a shelf of records and CDs and noticed a lot of heavy metal names. She didn't care for metal, but he had a Misfits album. One of her favorites. Maybe he's a cool old guy, she thought. Maybe he used to be in a band.

Some of the few new things in the house were a laptop set up next to a camera with a cord between them. The man also had a decent television with two worn recliner chairs in front of it. An orange cat perched on the arm of a chair, watching her.

"When we get downstairs, you can meet the real artist," the man said.

"You mean you're not Nevercore?" Eli asked.

"That moniker was thought of by my kid brother. If anyone is Nevercore, it's him. I'm just Bob."

Maddy didn't know why she hadn't thought of it 15 yards ago, but Bob's hands were wrinkled and hairless.

When Bob reached the basement door, a sharp metallic click cut through the humming quiet. When he stepped out of sight and Eli stepped after, Maddy looked for a lock on the door. A deadbolt.
The latch was on the outside of the door so that if one was locked in the basement, they would need a key to get out.

The temperature dropped as they ascended. "Say, you kids look young. How old are you?" "Seventeen," Eli answered.

"Your parents know where you are?"

"Yes," Maddy butted in, clear concise, yes, "We gave them your address so they could help us with directions. We don't come to Gresham much."

Eli rolled his eyes at Safety First Madison, but she knew she was in the right.

The basement was lit with single bare bulbs controlled by tattered strings. The lights stayed contained with nowhere to reflect.
The surfaces were dull and dusty, painted with tacky grays and browns. The wood beams, tables, and shelves were old, porous planks with years of dust dead on the surface.

Nevercore stood with his back to them, a familiar body with his shirt off. They now knew that his body hair extended to his back as well. Perhaps this was how he could weather the basement chill. He stood in front of an old wooden shop table that had seen decades of use. No doubt, it was ingrained with the chemical smells of his trade- smells that perhaps overcame the smells of decomposition. The area around him had actually been cleaned, it seemed. The shop table had been oiled and wiped clean and the floor actually shined around his feet. Next to the table was a big sink, surely not as white as it once was, but free from blemishes. Maddy imagined that workspace was probably covered in guts often enough that you'd have to have some good cleaning habits or else you'd have flies and maggots.

"Well, now, don't be rude. We have guests that are interested in buying a 'coon skull and want to shop around. They're just kids." Nevercore turned from his project. He wore a fox mask, but the eye holes were enlarged to reach his human sockets. He gestured toward a heavy utility shelf where his projects were on display before he turned back to his table.

"He don't talk much. A bit of a grump," Bob joked.

Maddy tried to see what Nevercore was working on, but it was obscured by his body.

Eli stepped towards the shelf and examined rows of individual bones stripped clean and lined up like a cartoon xylophone. The squirrel that they had seen on the website was on display as well. Eli picked it up and pointed it at Maddy.

"Look familiar, Mad?" he asked. He gave a gravelly voice to the squirrel, "I'm coming for you, Maddy! I'll be in your dreams!"

"Stop," she said. Eli frowned at the worry in her voice, but before he could apologize Nevercore was lifting the squirrel from Eli's hands and placing it on the shelf.

Eli looked after him, "Hey, I'm sorry. I wasn't making fun. The squirrel is really cool."

Nevercore had left his workspace exposed. On the table there was a lump with red and fur and bits of white.

Eli approached the items again, but this time more delicately. He stroked the surface of a skull with fierce teeth.

"This one's cool. What animal is it?"

He turned to get an answer from Nevercore, but Nevercore was back to work.

"That one's a coyote," Bob answered, "Shot it myself with a .22 when it was prowling around our house at night." "Did you eat it?" Eli asked.

"Sure. It wasn't exactly filet mignon, but if it's good enough for Lewis and Clark, it's good enough for me."

"Do any of the animals taste good?" Eli asked.

"We're fond of rabbit around here. They make a nice meal, especially when your disability check doesn't get you to the end of the month."

Their disability wasn't discernable to Maddy, but she knew it was impolite to ask about it.

Floor boards creaked overhead. When Maddy looked up curiously Bob explained that it was just the cat, Penny, named for her copper color.

"Ain't nobody else home unless we have a ghost," Bob said with a guffaw.

"Hey, are those human skulls?" Eli asked.

Maddy looked to the other side of the basement. Another shelf was partially obscured by an old curtain. Nevercore snapped his gaze to Bob.

"Sure are," Bob said, "Neat, aren't they?"

"We were actually wondering how people acquired human skulls.
Is it legal?" Eli asked.

"Yes," Bob answered, "but you have to buy them from other countries. Like India. They'll send a human skull over to the states."

"But who were these people?" Maddy asked.

"Don't know," Bob said, "but they were probably homeless or prisoners or something. Medical students use dead homeless people for research all the time."

"Can I pick one up?" Eli asked.

"Help yourself," Bob said. Bob slipped his hands into his pockets and rocked back on his feet with a friendly smile. "Babes in toyland, huh?" he said to Nevercore's back. Nevercore had his arms flexed and was pulling two things apart which produced a sticky peeling sound.

Eli lifted a skull with both hands and turned it over.

"It's so crazy to think that I have one of these under my skin. And that this was in a person for their whole life. So much happened in here," Eli said, "Ideas, memories, illusions. Our heads are amazing."

While Eli drank in his moment, Maddy glanced at the exit route.

"Hey, I gotta get going Eli. You getting a skull or what?"

"I'll tell you what," Bob said extending a coyote skull, "Take this one on the house. And why don't you all come back sometime. Perhaps when you're both 18."

Nevercore made a sound for the first time since they had been there. He let out an amused grunt as though he couldn't help it.

For the first time, Eli frowned.

"Let's go," Maddy said. She put one foot on the bottom step.

Eli stepped forward and reached a trembling hand out not going any nearer to Bob than he needed to. Bob made no effort to ease their discomfort or get the skull nearer to Eli's hand. Nevercore joined Bob by his side, took the skull, and transferred it to Eli's outstretched hand. Their eyes met and in Eli's periphery, he swore he saw incisors whittled to points in his greasy smile.

Maddy had a good view of his current project. The fur didn't look like any fur she had ever seen, though. It looked delicate and thin and like it didn't have a grain. It appeared to be longer than any hair she had seen on a wild animal or even a pet. She tore her eyes away when Eli was at her back giving her a push forward.

They were stomping up the stairs and sprinting through the house half expecting a trap or a locked front door. This time, Maddy didn't notice a record collection or a TV. It was death everywhere. Pelts, mounted heads, a fly banging his head on the window. Penny leapt up from a chair snatching the fly away into her maw.

After shooting out the front door, Maddy fumbled with her keys. "Ohmygodohmygodohmygod, letsgo."

Inside the car, they locked the doors. A creaking sound revealed Bob sauntering onto the front porch with his arms crossed on his chest. Maddy was trying to remove her boot, but gave up. She used her whole leg to press on the gas. They weren't safe to breathe until the house was out of sight.

***

During the ride home Maddy was too stunned to speak as she reviewed the images of Nevercore's home in her mind.

At Eli's house, Maddy joined him in his room stepping over piles of clothes. He lowered the skull into the terrarium and pressed it gently into the dirt. Sparky scuttled towards the skull and stopped short as if he was only smelling it.

"It looks perfect," Eli said.

"I guess. I don't know. I'm still shaking. Those were the scariest people I've ever met," Maddy said, "Like call-the-cops scary. Why did they say to come back when we're 18?"

"I don't know why you're so on edge. They were scary, but maybe it's kind of awesome. I guess the question is, were they being scary on purpose?"

The End.

The Road to Big Sur

G.D McFetridge

Physician: Dr. Lichten
642S-SED41

Last Monday morning I woke up with a brutal headache and I knew something had to change, so I flushed all the blue and white capsules down the toilet. They floated like little lifejackets while the vortex of swirling water took them down. I'd been taking pills for so long I couldn't even remember how long I'd been taking them … one in the morning and another one at night. On and on. The doctors said I had to take them because there was a bad genome somewhere in my brain. Yeah, right …

The first few days were pretty weird, but by the weekend everything cleared up and I could think again. I came back to life and decided to celebrate my newfound freedom by treating myself to a long drive up the coast. The Pacific Ocean was windswept. Blue as a crystal and the sky diamond clear. I felt strong and free … I'd never been better.

That afternoon, about forty miles south of Big Sur, I spotted a young hitchhiker and I thought about stopping but I guess the mood wasn't right. She looked unkempt and she was smoking a cigarette. I hate women who smoke.

Nearing the mountain range south of Big Sur, I noticed clouds gathering in the northwest, and the sea had turned choppy and rough. I checked the gas gauge—the needle was at the quarter-full mark. "The van's sure getting good mileage," I said, because I like talking to myself when I'm feeling happy and light in my burden. Then, as if by some bizarre coincidence, the engine suddenly sputtered and died. I coasted off the road, parked on the dirt shoulder and tapped the gas gauge with my finger. It still said a quarter-full, but after several more thumps the needle jarred loose and settled below the empty mark.

I remembered the road sign a couple miles back. It had said Big Sur was only six miles and so I put my jacket on and locked the van, and then walked up the winding highway, hoping to flag a ride to a gas station. Ten minutes later the highway sloped over a rise into a dense pine forest. Twilight was fading and an uneasy feeling shivered up my spine. There were strange sounds and I was sure some large animal was watching me from the darkness of the woods.

I heard the sound of a distant car engine and tires gripping pavement. Headlights flashed as the vehicle swung through a curve. A moment later an old station wagon pulled over and stopped, and I saw two heads silhouetted against the glow of headlights. The driver was a husky man with a beard. He got out and met me as I approached the car.

"That your yellow van back there?" he asked.

"Yeah, I ran out of gas."

"I'll give you a ride to Big Sur, but I can't say for sure if any gas stations are still open. They close early on Sundays." He motioned to the back of the car. "Might be easier if you climbed in the tailgate, the back seat's full of junk and old newspapers."

"Thanks," I said and crawled inside. There was another man sitting in the passenger seat. He glanced over his shoulder. His head was shaved head but I couldn't see his face very well. He didn't say anything. I scrunched in between an old television and a tricycle that was missing its front wheel, next to a large wooden box full of what looked like used toilet and plumbing parts.

The driver shut the door and the light went off. When we got back on the highway, they started passing a pint bottle back and forth and talking about some claptrap hunting trip. I could smell the alcohol, and the driver said something about how he'd got him an eight-point buck in them White Mountains, out in Nevada. The other man took a swig and had his own story about a thousand-pound elk he'd shot the year before.

"But shit, I didn't have no elk tag," he said, "so when I saw that sonofabitch game warden roaring up the canyon in his jeep, I just cut out the liver and got the hell out of there. The fine for no tag is fifteen hundred bucks … can you fucking believe it?"

I didn't like the sound of the story because it seemed ugly and senseless. Then something spooky came over me, like a cold sweat combined with a tingling sensation, and I had to catch my breath. I was a prisoner inside the station wagon. No way to get out.

The man in the passenger seat glanced over his shoulder as if maybe he'd heard my thoughts or something, and then he leaned over to the bearded man and said something in a low voice. They were making plans. The driver grunted and took another swig from the bottle. I was anxious and my palms were sweating but I told myself that I was imagining things. But then I remembered the news blurb I'd heard on the radio, how the police were looking for serial killers who picked up hitchhikers, and they suspected the killers had also beaten an attendant to death in an all-night convenience store just south of Monterey. How could I let myself get into a situation like this?

I could handle myself in a fight all right, but if they had guns or something, I'd be out of luck. Or if they were tough guys, I probably couldn't take them both. The driver was about my height but a lot huskier, and I didn't really get much of a look at the other guy. But one thing was certain, there was something cruel and vicious in the tone of his voice.

I was thinking how much farther can it be to Big Sur? Because I still remembered the road sign and that we'd already been driving for at least ten minutes. Maybe they'd taken a turnoff I hadn't notice. I craned my head and looked out the windshield, but a wall of dark forest surrounded the winding road. My heart started pounding and I couldn't get my breath. It was the same feeling I had when I was ten years old, when an older girl in the neighborhood ask me if I wanted to climb into an old freezer inside her dad's storage shed, one with a door that opened like a coffin lid. She said the locking mechanism had been removed and it was safe to get inside.

"I can do it," she boasted. She hopped up and climbed in and closed the freezer door. It was kind of spooky for a moment but then she sprang out like a jack-in-the-box.

"See, Billy, it's safe and we could even get inside together and … well, you know…" she said, giving me a coy look. She was twelve and had long red hair, and sometimes we'd sneak up in her brother's tree fort and she'd show me what was under her dress.

"Now you get inside," she said.

"I thought we were going to get inside together."

She gave me a cross look. "I might let you touch it this time, but first you have to show me how brave you are and get in by yourself. You have to close the door all the way."

My palms were sweating, but I climbed cautiously into the old freezer and then tested my arm strength against the weight of the door. It was easy and I could get out if I wanted, so I squatted down and let the door close until there was just a small crack of light. But then I got scared and didn't want to let the door close all the way, but before I could push it open, she lept on top the freezer.

Everything went black, a blackness so heavy and overpowering it felt as if it were sucking the life out of me. My heart exploded inside my chest and I gasped for air, frantically pushing upward to open the door. But she was too heavy and all I could do was scream.

I was suddenly afraid that she would lock the freezer door and leave me there to suffocate. She was a monster and I couldn't do anything; all I could do was scream louder and louder. And when that didn't work I cried and cried, begging her to open the door.

I don't know how long she kept me inside the freezer—maybe it was only ten seconds, though it seemed like an eternity—and when the door finally opened a wonderful light washed over me and I could breathe again. My God I could breathe …

"You're such a little pussy," she said, pointing at me. "Crybaby! Crybaby!"

I was so relieved I felt grateful and wanted to thank her for setting me free and sparing my life, but then a switch went off inside my head and everything became blurred and fuzzy, dark around the edges. All I saw was her finger pointed in my face and her face twisted in mocking laughter, and I wanted to beat her, pound her mouth and nose with my fists, bludgeon her skull with a baseball bat.

Just then the station wagon hit a pothole and jarred me loose from the dark memory. The two men were talking again in hushed voices. I knew what they were planning. I patted my hand over objects in the back of the station wagon. There were rags and an empty oil can, pieces of pipe and another can full of nails … and the pipe wrench. I picked it up and set it in my lap—it was cold and heavy. The driver took another pull off the bottle and I knew I had to move fast. Had to shove the television aside and scramble over the back seat and hit the passenger in the head with the pipe wrench. Then I'd go after the driver and make him pull over. I'd beat him unconscious. Adrenaline was pumping into my arteries like a broken waterline. I pushed the television out of my way and leaned over the rear seat but the station wagon suddenly braked and pulled hard to the left. I fell forward, headfirst between the front and back seats.

"Sorry, slick, didn't mean to throw you so hard," the driver said and laughed. "This is where we turn off. I'm gonna let you out now. There's a gas station about three-hundred yards up the road. Maybe they're still open."

The station wagon rolled to a stop and the driver opened his door. The dome light came on and I carefully set the pipe wrench to the floor, pretending I was rubbing my leg. He walked around to the back and opened the tailgate.

"You all right?" he asked.

I climbed out quick and said, "I'm fine … sorry for knocking that box over."

"Hell, don't worry about it, it's just a bunch of junk anyway." I watched the station wagon bounce down the gravel road, and the taillights disappeared into the darkness. "That was close, that was too close," I whispered to myself. But I couldn't understand why they had changed their minds.

The night air was colder, with only a few patches of starlight between the clouds above the canopy of tall pines, and it felt like rain was coming. Around the next bend in the road there was a faint glow, and as I cleared the sweeping curve I spotted a lighted gas station with a car parked next to one of the pumps. An attendant with overalls and a baseball cap was standing at the rear of the car.

"I ran out of gas a few miles south," I said, out of breath. "Would it be possible to buy or borrow a gas can?"

There was a shiny chrome-plated tire iron on top the gas pump, and it seemed like an odd place for a tire iron. She shook her head. "We don't sell no gas cans and the boss says we can't lend none out. You'd better try the general store." She pointed up the dark road.

"How far is it?"

"Less than a quarter-mile," she said. Then she removed the nozzle from the car's tank and walked to the driver's side window. The man said something and handed her a couple twenties. The engine started and he pulled out onto the road and disappeared around the bend.

"How much longer you open?" I asked.

"Usually I close right about now, but I'll wait until you get back. Just hurry it up, because it's getting really cold," she said, and crossed her arms over her chest.

I looked at her for a second and smiled. She was cute, thick red hair, pale skin and freckles. She smiled back and gave me a special look, and I knew that look because I'd seen it before. I always knew that look. It was something you could tell in their eyes, you could tell that they liked you and that maybe ... well, you know what I mean. But the next thing I remembered was a crack of thunder and the sound of rain, a hard rain, and I was running and everything swirled around me, blurry and dark. Shadows spilled across the cold highway. I was breathing hard and running down the road with a gas can in one hand and a tire iron in the other. I tossed the tire iron over the guardrail into a deep ravine.

The following day I was in Carmel, eating a burger and some fries and listening to the radio in my van. The serial killers had struck again. Some poor girl who worked at a gas station in Big Sur got herself murdered ... go figure. I'll bet it was those drunken rednecks who gave me the ride. Something about them didn't add up, something was scary about them, particularly the man with the shaved head. I'm just lucky I got away.

"Maybe I'll head north to Oregon for a while," I said. I was checking myself in the rearview mirror. Because I like talking to myself when I feel happy, and Portland is a real nice town.

The End.

Bestselling Horror US

1 Run - *Blake Crouch*

2   Abandon - *Blake Crouch*

3   The Remaining - *D.J. Molles*

4   The Remaining: Refugees - *D.J. Molles*

5   The Remaining: Aftermath - *D.J. Molles*

6   Apocalypse Z: The Beginning of the End - *M. Loureiro and P. Carmell*

7   Huntress Moon (The Huntress/FBI Thrillers) - *Alexandra Sokoloff*

8   Omega Days - *John L. Campbell*

9   Better Off Dead in Deadwood - *Ann Charles and C.S. Kunkle*

10   Long Time Coming - *Edie Claire*

Compiled May 1st - May 31st 2013
Amazon.com Kindle Chart

Bestselling Horror UK

1 The Wanderer in Unknown Realms - *John Connolly*

2 Eerie - *Jordan Crouch and Blake Crouch*

3 Huntress Moon (The Huntress/FBI Thrillers) - *Alexandra Sokoloff*

4 Asylum: The Complete Series - *Amy Cross*

5 NorthWest (Book II) - *J.H. Glaze, J.H. Glaze and Susan Grimm*

6 World War Z - *Max Brooks*

7 The Scarlet Tessera - *Julian Lorr*

8 The Detective Megapack - *Various Authors*

9 Slouching Towards Kowloon - *Alison Ripley*

10 A Good and Useful Hurt - *Aric Davis*

Compiled May 1st - May 31st 2013
Amazon.co.uk Kindle Chart

Group
Therapy
06.13
25 Years in Black, Zombie
Evacuation Races! and
plague spreading.

"The world has gone to hell! Surely zombies are to blame....right?"

It may have been out for over a year but Plague by Ndemic games has not only been picked up by many iPad, iPhone and android users, it was also voted App store Best of 2012. So we wanted to share the love and cover what is so great about this game.

Well (and don't be mad) it doesn't revolve around a zombie outbreak to start. Plague Inc begins off nice enough, you choose a country that you want to infect with your virus. From here you slowly build up your DNA blocks until you have enough to "mutate" the strain. This is done in a nice clean interface that even on the iPhone you can easily see what the effects will be and how it can help or hinder your growth.

For example, picking to improve water transmission if you are in a warm country that uses boats as a main transport option is a good start. Over time the choices build up and as your plague spreads around the world - it will start to get noticed. This is where the challenge comes in, the more people who die the more the governments want to stop you / it. I should of mentioned that at the start of each game you have to name your plague. I couldn't help calling mine 1Direction....

So once "1D" has started to be noticed and the cure percentage creeps up, its time to evolved some protection. This is carried out in the same fashion as evolving your symptoms, but this time you are building up specific resilience. As the game plays out there will be times when the cure is a little ahead, the fun is trying to mutate the plague to stop them.

The game can be picked up and played in around 30 minutes but if you really want to destroy every living human, you can almost double the playing time. There are several "levels" that you can unlock so there is a lot of replay value. The graphics really help with the enjoyment of the game, the boats and planes moving around the map and the fact that you can zoom in to specific regions just make it really slick.

Overall the past 12 months of this games life has seen it go from strength to strength and long may it continue.

See, still no zombies....

Requirements: Compatible with iPhone, iPod touch and iPad. Requires iOS 4.3 or later. This app is optimized for iPhone 5.

www.ndemiccreations.com

Cover Art

We have had a letter in from a horror fan and it made us think about our covers and the way women are depicted in the genre.
Over the years the role of the female (mainly in films) has been that of eye candy and a character that "needs to be saved." It's nice to see that this has moved on and we are getting scream queens coming through and "last girls" that really kick ass.

The letter highlighted that the imagery of our preview issue might be a little strong and may put some readers off. So with that in mind we will be having male and female models on the cover of Sanitarium in the near future. We will however not lose our nod to Poe with the eyes being crossed out.

We hope you enjoy the upcoming issues and if you have any comments or questions please feel free to email us.

Thank you for supporting us and horror as a genre.

Barry Skelhorn

"If you go down to the woods today..."

October is going to be a busy month for many horror fans, parties to attended, movie marathons and maybe a little haunted house visiting. But what if you want to get fit whilst maintaining your horror fix?

Jon Ford, Race Director.

Well this is where the team behind the Zombie Evacuation Race come in.

"Locals have been reporting hearing strange noises at night after a recent laboratory break-in in the area. Police say they are working hard to recover the stolen samples but assure the public that the samples were harmless and do not pose a threat to the general public.

Whilst the Government has thus far refused to confirm officially, the breached laboratory is rumoured to be one near Bassingbourn, a location that has been under heavy quarantine since the events of October 27th 2012.

Citizens in the area are reporting seeing a large number of soldiers and equipment from what is rumoured to be the Royal Armoured Zombie Outbreak Response team (RAZOR) in the area, prompting speculation that just one year after so many died at the hands of a plague of the undead, Cambridgeshire is once again about to be declared unsafe."

Course Type:

Mostly Flat - Trees, Grass, Mud, Road mix.

"Just days after news of the recent outbreak in Cambridge the Government has now confirmed that the country is once again in the grip of an outbreak of what they are calling 'Infection X'. This is the same infection that led to large areas of land in Cambridge and Pippingford being evacuated and 'cleansed' by the army in 2012.

Information is now detailing an outbreak north of the border in Scotland around the Edinburgh region. It is unknown at this point how the Infection managed to spread so far North. It has prompted a full scale National Emergency Alert.

In response the Emergency Services and the Army have begun to mobilise and evacuations are now taking place across the country in many of the major cities close to the identified areas of infection.

Citizens are being advised to leave behind non-essential items

and make their way to the nearest RAZOR (Royal Armoured Zombie Outbreak Response) evacuation point in the affected areas."

Course Type:

Hilly and muddy, field and forest

"The Government addressed the country today in an attempt to reassure the general public and calm fears of a repeat of the events of 2012. They have announced that the Armed Forces have successfully culled the number of infected, or zombies as they are becoming more commonly known as.

However scepticism is rife as reports come out of Cambridgeshire of thousands of casualties, and information trickles down out of Scotland reporting that the Edinburgh area has been surrounded and torched.

More worrying for the general public however is that reports are coming in of the infection spreading to more areas of the country. Advance reports suggest that RAZOR (Royal Armoured Zombie Outbreak Response) is mobilising towards Pippingford again, one of the sites of last year's outbreaks. Reports are also coming in about huge smoke plumes climbing into the sky from the Bristol area. Eye witnesses say that this smoke is coming from a number of mass body burnings in the city and surrounding areas."

Course Type:
Flat fields, some forestation

"Despite Government officials claiming huge success for the Army last week in driving the infected out of the Bristol area, news today is grim, with numerous agencies reporting seeing vehicles from the specialised RAZOR (Royal Armoured Zombie Outbreak Response) team flooding into the Pippingford area as conventional and territorial Army units retreat after sustaining high causalities.

It is rumoured that an infected solider bypassed the medical checks and caused an outbreak within the barracks, quickly overwhelming the forces there who were unprepared for such an event. London local new services are listing the casualty rate at almost 90%.

Experts who specialise in the spread of infectious diseases are now predicting that this may be the countries last chance to successfully stop the epidemic from spreading any further and if efforts fall short this weekend, then the entire United Kingdom will need to be quarantined in order to prevent the infection spreading globally."

Course Type:
Hills and heavy forestation. Some field.

Will you be part of the problem or will you run for the sake of humanity?

The Zombie Evacuation Race is a 5km interactive obstacle course race in which Evacuee's run for their lives while Zombies try to infect them.

Evacuee's will be given a belt that contains 3 LifeTags which must be worn fully visible. These tags are attached to the belts by velcro and as such can be torn off if grabbed by a hungry Zombie. The aim of the Evacuee is to navigate the 5km course and get to the finish line with at least one of their LifeTags left on their belt.

On their way around the course they will be challenged by differing terrain, different route choices and a variety of themed obstacles intended to plunge them into the experiences of their favourite Zombie TV Shows and Movies and slow down their progress and make them easy meat for their living dead pursuers.

If they get to the Evacuation Point with one of their LifeTags intact then they'll be classified and rewarded as a SURVIVOR. If they lose their LifeTags, then they'll be written off as infected.

Regardless of their status everyone is timed around the course and prizes are available for the fastest male, female and team.

The Zombies on the course are all willing volunteers who love to COSPlay and act as Zombies for the day. Whether they want to sit, shuffle, lurch or run we can find a role for them on our event.

The Zombie Evacuation Race is a NON-CONTACT SPORT. As such the Zombies can not touch the Evacuees, only grab for their Life Tags as the Evacuees try to dodge past them. Conversely the Evacuee's cannot touch the Zombies, the infection is contagious so the aim of the course is to DODGE the Zombies, not force their way past.

If you would like more informtion regarding costs and signup, please head over to the office website:

https://zombieevacuation.com/

Or head over to their facebook page and hang out with fellow runners before the main events.

https://www.facebook.com/zombieevacuation

For most there are plays that have stood the test of time, tens of thousands if not millions have passed through their doors and have been entertained, moved and some have even shocked and scared during the performance. There is one however that seems timeless and almost as if it was penned back in the Victorian era, however this play was based on a book written in the early 1980's.

The Woman in Black by Susan Hill was first published by Hamish Hamilton in 1983. The story centres on a young solicitor, Arthur Kipps who is summoned to Crythin Gifford, a small market town on the north east coast of the United Kingdom to attend the funeral of Mrs Alice Drablow. She was an elderly recluse widow who lived alone in the desolate and secluded Eel Marsh House.

Along the way we meet several characters who have their own thoughts and experiences of Eel Marsh House. The history is revealed as the truth is slowly stripped away from the legend and the townsfolk whispers. The book, around 192 pages is worth a read - especially if you find yourself on a cold windswept evening on the Norfolk Broads like I did - Ed.

The stage play stays true to the book with a few changes, it was adapted by Stephen Mallatratt. In this adaptation an older Kipps enlists a young actor to help him tell the story of the "Woman in Black", hoping that the telling of his tale will help him move on and rid him of the memory. The story continues with the actor playing the part of your Kipps, whist the real Kipps plays the roles of the people he met.

The staging of the play lends itself well to the theatre that currently holds it. The Fortune Theatre in Covent Garden has run the play since 1989. Making it the second longest running stage play in London - second only to "The Mousetrap". Ironically over the years it has had its share of ghostly sightings of a "Woman in Black".

One such account was during a performance. One of the actors, Sebastian Harcombe, saw two women to the right of the stage where no living person was in fact standing. At the same time, the leading lady mentioned that she felt that she had been followed onto the stage by someone she couldn't see.

This coupled with the smaller stall layout, overall number of seats, the acoustics and gothic nature of the play. It really does set the atmosphere for this great story. It is comforting that over the years there have been many re-telling of classic tales on the stage, Dracula, Frankenstein and more recently the successful "Ghost Stories" to bring horror to the forefront. But when you have a legacy like "the Woman in Black" that has toured worldwide, in countless languages for the past 25 years, who knows who and what it will inspire in the future.

The Woman in Black is soon to enter its summer schedule and will have 8pm showings Monday - Saturday from the 22nd July to the 24th August. Matinees will be shown during this period on Tuesdays at 3pm and 4pm on Saturdays. Tickets range from £18 for Upper Circle to £48.00 for the Stalls the Fortune Theatre is around 5 a minute walk from Covent Garden underground station.

http://www.thewomaninblack.com/

Fortune Theatre, Russell Street, Covent Garden, WC2B 5HH

Tricks, Mischief, and Mayhem
By Daniel I. Russell
Review by Casey Chaplin

Before Reviewing a collection of shorts is never easy. There are many different factors to take into account, such as style, theming, and overall quality of each story. In the past when I've done a review of an anthology, I was able to write a small blurb about each tale and give a brief thought on it. In the case of Daniel I. Russell's Tricks, Mischief, and Mayhem, that would be near impossible in such a short time. So instead I'll give an overall opinion, and point out a favourite.

First though, I should mention that this is more of a "Best of" collection. All of these stories have been printed or published elsewhere in the past, and are now being brought together by Crystal Lake Publishing to be enjoyed as a group, so if you're a fan of Russell's work, there's a good chance you've already read a few, if not all, of these stories.

One thing I noticed about this collection is that it plays on a lot of morals. I was able to find a semblance of lesson in each story, but whether or not that was intentional, I cannot say. However it made reading the stories a tad more interesting at the start. Later on though, it became a bit tedious. I found myself wondering what the next moral was going to be. Would it be that revenge is not the answer, or that one should respect Mother Nature? It almost felt as if Russell was trying to pound home a message using horror, which isn't a bad thing, but in large doses, 21 to be exact, it became a little difficult to swallow.

Another issue I felt this collection had was that there wasn't enough to them. Yes, they're shorts, but that doesn't mean we can't have a back story of some kind, or at least a bit of information, a hint even, as to why the terror is occurring. Not every story did this, but a few did and it left a very unsatisfied feeling when it was all said and done.

Nevertheless, one story that stood out for me was By the Banks of the Nabarra. This is a tale of domestic abuse that goes on for too long, and the wife, Melissa, decides to take the matter into her own hands. However things start to go awry when an ancient native folktale is brought to life. The story is well written and most importantly gives context to the events. It involves an easily relatable protagonist, and a villain so filled with hate that it's easy to loath him. This narrative was by far the stand out of the lot.

In conclusion, I cannot say for certain that these stories in particular were the best to group together. By the end it felt a little preachy with the lessons that seemed to be constantly there, as well the lack of context in a few of them as well was a bit off putting. With all that said, Daniel I. Russell isn't a bad author, in fact he's very talented, I just feel that this collection fell a bit short.

VERDICT: 48%

Sleepers
By Paul Kane
Review by Casey Chaplin

Often thrown about is the phrase The city that never sleeps. It usually means New York, or in a fictional universe, the core metropolis with the dense population and the 24 hour work schedule with a never ending hustle and bustle. But a term that isn't thrown around all too often is The city that always sleeps, and that's more or less what Paul Kane's Sleepers is all about. It's a situation that starts off fairly harmlessly, just a couple in a doctor's office having a routine check up due to some excessive tiredness. From there an epidemic ensues leaving the small city of Middletown reeling.

The story leads you in with a sense of no real antagonist as the epidemic of this sleeping disease spreads rapidly, but thankfully that changes as the book progresses. We are quickly introduced to a Microbiologist called Andrew Strauss and his assistant Bridget, the former seemingly being the only hope the city, maybe even the world has to cure this mysterious outbreak. It just so happens that this particular pandemic is exactly what Dr. Strauss has been looking for - a sleeping contagion that will lead him to the literal girl of his dreams. She is a girl that he sees in his reoccurring dreams, and in his mind, is also the key to solving the viral outbreak.

Kane's style of writing comes out again this work, much like it did in his previous Creakers. His very simple but effect portrayal of characters worked wonders in Creakers and lead to a great experience. Although that work was substantially shorter than Sleepers, it made me want to read more, and I finished it seemingly as soon as I started it. However, I cannot say that was the case with Sleepers. I didn't find myself able to connect to the story, or the characters like I had previous with Creakers. Reading it wasn't a chore, but it lacked something. The story was perhaps too grand for what the writing offered, and maybe Kane wasn't knowledgeable enough on the topics for which he was writing. But that happens, not everybody is a Military General or a Microbiologist - however I feel that more research would have benefited to help fill in the details.

I don't want to say though, that no research was done when writing this book. He did add snippets of terms and whatnot in the story, but it felt like it was just added in for the sake of it; I would have loved for some of the terms to have been expanded upon, if nothing more than for emersions sake. With all that in mind, I have to say that Sleepers was a distinctly average read. The story felt like it was done before, and it has been. Perhaps not the sleeping concept, but the idea of some sort of plague outbreak has been seen in many different forms. Movies such as Blindness and Outbreak leap to mind, and even the blockbuster flop The Happening all play with this same idea.

All in all, Sleepers isn't a bad read, as I said, just don't go in with massive expectations of an apocalyptic epic and perhaps you'll enjoy it more than I did.

About Casey Chaplin:

Casey Chaplin is a horror writer, reviewer, and content creator. He has written a full length horror novel entitled Lizzy; competed several screenplays for production, and writes reviews for various websites and magazines including Gamers Mantra and Sanitarium Magazine. He has an education in Radio Broadcasting, with a major in Creative Writing and has worked both full time and freelance for several radio stations.

Her Unremembering Way / The Bell Witch by John F.D Taff
Double Dragon Publishing
Review by Rob Salem

"Her Unremembering Way" is author John F. D. Taff's retelling of one of the most famous ghost stories of American folklore. Based on the true events surrounding the Bell family of Tennessee in the early 1800's, Taff uses known facts about the Bell Witch legend to weave a story that explores the Bell family and possible causes for the haunting.

Taff has clearly done his research in early 19th century American history, as well as in the Bell Witch story itself. He pays attention to small details that help bring the setting to life, which serves to provide historical context for the story as well as set the stage for certain elements of the story itself. History itself almost becomes a character in the story and not merely just a backdrop that is irrelevant to the story being told. The reader is given a small but accurate look into daily life in rural Tennessee in the early 1800's, in a way that matters to the legend of the Bell Witch.

Taff's narrative is clear and descriptive with enough detail to offer the reader some immersion, yet not so much that the story is bogged down by too much exposition. The pacing is well done, with the scenes changing in much the same way as movie might. The author does well at creating tension by giving the reader a slow build up, teasing with ominous hints about what is to come. Even being familiar with the Bell Witch legend, I found myself reading on, slightly apprehensive about what was going to happen – this rings as a mark of success in Taff's writing style. That said though, there were moments where it was hard to follow the dialogue (which this book is heavy with); sometimes there were more than two characters interacting, and while Taff attempted to create naturally moving conversations, in print certain identifiers are needed to clearly indicate who is speaking.

"Her Unremembering Way" is a worthwhile read for anyone interested the Bell Witch legend, American folklore, or just a good old-fashioned ghost story. While there isn't anything overtly new or original with the story being told, the author does well at telling his version of this story. By and large I found the Witch to be the most interesting character, while finding it difficult to invest myself into any of the other characters. With this version of the Bell Witch legend, Taff has told a good ghost story – he hasn't reinvented the wheel or created some shocking new twist to try and catch readers off guard; rather, he's breathed a little fresh life into an American legend while taking the reader down a well-worn and familiar path. While readers shouldn't be looking for some new bits of historical fact or grand revelation into such a well-known tale, what they will find is a well written and entertaining version of that tale, one worth reading over the course of a couple evenings.

VERDICT: 80%

Classics Review:
The Doom Of The Griffiths
By Elizabeth Gaskell
Review by Rob Salem

Published in 1858, "The Doom Of The Griffiths" is a Gothic tale by Elizabeth Gaskell. This short story tells the tale of the fall of the Griffith family of Wales, the victim of a curse brought about by ancestral sins. Mrs. Gaskell was a prolific British writer of the Victorian era, producing more than 40 works during the course of her early 19th century life. While she wasn't strictly a ghost-story writer, much of her popularity came from those stories, which are all written in the Gothic theme. "The Doom Of The Griffiths" is a wonderful example of Gothic storytelling, and as with other early Gothic authors, shows where the foundations of Gothic horror were laid a couple hundred years ago.

True to the Gothic theme, "The Doom Of The Griffiths" captures the aspect of the tragic love story and weaves it together with the classic ghost story and the family haunted and ultimately fallen by the sins of ancestors of generations long past. However, much like her other writing, Mrs. Gaskell uses the story as a sort of social commentary (she was noted for using her work to describe the plight of women in Victorian England), the primary example of such here being the difference in social status and how it affected such things as love and family.

In reviewing previous classic works, I've often described the writing as perhaps a bit difficult for the modern reader, and this work is no different. The simple fact is that language has changed over the past 200 years – except among certain social groups, much of the eloquence of the speech of the Victorian and Edwardian eras has been lost. Large, educated vocabularies have given way to over-simplified slang and laziness, and words have been allowed to have lost some of their deeper meanings, which are too often referred to nowadays as "archaic." What has happened is that the works of the Victorian authors sometimes read for the modern reader as a tangled and overly verbose web of forgotten words and uncomfortable phrasing; unfortunately, this also means that there's a good chance that the late 20th and early 21st century readers probably miss much of the depth of the writing. Mrs. Gaskell's work is no different in this regard.

"The Doom Of The Griffiths" is a subtle sort of ghost story, speaking more of the ghosts that hang over the Griffith family in the form of an ancient family curse than of spirits come back from the grave seeking vengeance or to otherwise haunt the living. Mrs. Gaskell's short story evokes a certain Shakespearean quality due to its plot, and in some regards comes across as a faint echo of

The Bard's "Hamlet" and "Macbeth." This story isn't as horrific in nature as some of the other works I've reviewed, being firmly rooted more in the tragic theme, but the subtle commentary in Mrs. Gaskell's eloquence begs the reader to independently explore topics that in her time certainly were horrific, and it is this psychological element that solidly marks "The Doom Of The Griffiths" as part of the foundation for what horror has become today.

About Rob Salem:

Rob Salem is a well-traveled poet and writer from Northern Indiana. He is lives in a quiet rural neighborhood with his wife and son. He spends his weekends participating in historically oriented hobbies, playing guitar, and enjoying good cigars and good beer.

CLAYTON HILL SANITARIUM

The Dust Storm

Ambrose Stolliker

Physician: Dr. Peterson
8268-WC729

Helen Stokely woke at the kitchen table with a start. A solitary candle provided the only light in the house. She looked at the clock. It was two in the afternoon. She'd slept for more than an hour, but did not feel rested. The muscles and joints of her thin body ached and it was hard to get in a decent breath. It's the dust. It's everywhere. She went to the medicine cabinet, took out a small bottle of Vaseline and dabbed some inside her nostrils and around the edges. She had done the same for the children not long before putting them to sleep. It was the only way to keep the sinuses clear of prairie dirt.

She went to dry her hands with a dish towel. As she did, she noticed her dress was still damp from giving the children their baths earlier that afternoon. Even with the drought, she gave them baths every day to wash the dust out of their eyes and hair. She went upstairs to change and then checked on the children. They were still asleep, even baby Abel, who'd only started sleeping through the night a few weeks before. She went back downstairs to see to the windows and doors.

Every window was glued shut and covered with damp bed sheets. It was all she could do to keep out the dust. The doors were more difficult. Wet towels at their bases helped somewhat, but the wind was so strong that sand inevitably found its way inside. She pulled back the sheet covering the kitchen window. Outside was almost complete blackness. Visibility was poor beyond the farmhouse's wrap-around porch, which was covered with several inches of dirt. She wondered where the soil had come from. Texas? Nebraska? Kansas? It didn't matter. The dust got into everything. There was no escaping it. All she could do was fight a seemingly never-ending war of attrition that she knew would end in defeat for her and her children.

The wind howled, interrupting Helen's train of thought. A cluster of tumbleweeds blew across the porch and were carried away into the darkness. She let the sheet fall back, deciding they would hold for now, and surveyed the kitchen. All the cupboards were open and bare, save for a few loaves of bread and dried beef. The beef had come from the last of the farm's emaciated cows. Her husband, Lucas, had slaughtered it several days before, only to find the animal's digestive tract full of dirt. Helen had almost cried when her children ate the beef and complained of grit getting stuck between their teeth.

The ice box was equally devoid of food with the exception of a stick of butter and some eggs that had probably gone over since the electricity was knocked out by the dust storm the week before. Helen closed it and went to the living room. As she went, she noticed the door to the basement was ajar and rushed to close it. Then, she propped a chair under the doorknob to keep it from opening again. Sometimes, the wind pushed pockets of air trapped in the cellar up the stairwell and blew the door open. *Yes, that's what must've happened.* On a lark, she picked up the telephone to see if service was back. Static buzzed in her ear and she put the receiver back in its resting place.

In the living room, all that remained of their furniture was a sofa and a small cherry table. Everything else had been sold off the year before to keep the bank from foreclosing on the farm. As it was, Lucas was six months behind in the mortgage. The dust had destroyed most of the wheat crop last season and they didn't have enough money to buy the seed for a new crop this year. It was over for the Stokelys in Oklahoma, but Lucas was too stubborn to admit defeat. *It's one of the things I love and hate about him.* She sat on the sofa and closed her eyes. *Dear God, Lucas, where are you? It's been a week. Don't you know we're dying without you?*

She played over the last week in her mind. *When did he take the Model T into Bull's Head? Monday? Tuesday? I can't remember. What day is it now? Wednesday, I think.* Abel had developed a cough that quickly turned into dust pneumonia, a condition that had already killed thousands of people – the elderly and children mostly – across the Southern Plains.

"Looks like there's a lull in the dust storm," Lucas had told her. "I'll go into Bull's Head and see if Doc O' Reilly'll come and take a look at the baby."

She'd begged him not to leave them, but he insisted.

"I'm not letting the flamin' dust take my baby boy," he'd said. Then, pecking her cheek, "Don't fret, woman. I'll be back 'fore the next duster hits."

With that, he'd gone. Not an hour later, the dust storm rolled in from the west.

On the table next to the sofa was a ten-day old copy of the *Bull's Head Bugle*. Helen picked it up and tried to read it just to pass the time, but the stories were the same as always. Wheat prices were at an all-time low. The banks were foreclosing on farms at a record rate. The drought was now in its fourth year and the Panhandle was already on pace to have even less rain than last year, which had also been an all-time low. Oklahoma was a parched land and soon, many said, it would be an abandoned one. Already, several of the cities around Bull's Head had turned into ghost towns. The prairie was emptying out of people. After a few minutes, Helen put the newspaper aside and closed her eyes.

Her thoughts turned to her mother and father in South Bend, Indiana. She'd written them a week before, begging for money, but with postal service at a standstill since the dust storm rolled in, she wondered if the letter had even left the post office in Bull's Head. Lucas had fought her tooth and nail not to send the letter, relenting only when it was clear they had no other choice. It hurt her heart to see the unmistakable glint of defeat in her husband's eyes. Coming to Oklahoma had been his idea. Helen hated the high plains. It was too hot and dry during the summer and too cold and windy during the winter. She stayed because she loved him.

Helen was about to doze again when she heard the baby crying. Upstairs, she sat down and nursed him. Burping him produced a thin stream of breast milk tainted with dark streaks of prairie dust. She cleaned him up and then held him close.

"Hold on, Abel. Pa's comin' back. He's comin' back, I promise."

Her eight-year-old daughter, Mary, appeared in the doorway. She was pale and thin. "You need somethin', mama?"

"No. You go wake Johnny and Lucille so we can make supper. Hurry along, now."

Downstairs, Helen put Abel in a crib and started on supper. A few minutes later, Mary appeared with Johnny and Lucille.

"Come here and help your mother," Helen said to Mary.

The girl obeyed, pouring glasses of water for everyone from the jugs Helen had filled at the well before the dust storm hit.

"When's pa comin' home, mama?" Johnny whined.

"I don't know. He's waitin' this duster out in Bull's Head. You be a big boy and stop that whinin'."

"What if he got caught in the storm on the way into town?" Mary asked.

Helen turned on her eldest daughter. "Don't say that. Your pa is fine."

Lucille decided to chime in on the conversation. "I want papa!" she yelled.

"Lucille Stokely, you stop that yellin'!" Lucille went silent.

"I don't think he's comin' back, like Willie Boynton's pa didn't come back when that big duster hit last year," Mary said, her voice low.

Helen couldn't take it anymore. She erupted. "Now just stop it! All of you! Your pa is fine and he's comin' back and I don't wanna hear anymore about it! That's final!"

Mary looked like she'd been slapped. Lucille's eyes filled with tears. Johnny started crying outright.

Helen turned back to preparing supper and let the children have their cries. When the last sniffles had come and gone, she brought the meager meal to the table and they all sat down and said grace. They ate in silence. Outside, the wind blew hard, forcing another air pocket up through the cellar. The cellar door rattled the chair under its knob.

"Why's the cellar all locked up, mama?" This was Mary.

"I don't want you children going down there. It's too dark and you might get hurt."

"What if we need something?"

"I said no. If someone needs to go down there, I'll go. Now hush up and finish your supper."

When they were done, Helen had Lucille and Johnny help Mary with the dishes while she tended to the baby in the living room. Like the other children, Abel was ashen, his eyes bloodshot. He coughed continuously, then cried. *Poor little thing, his throat's all torn up from coughin' so.* She whispered in his ear, then tried to soothe him with a lullaby, but Abel would not be consoled. Helen felt herself start to shake. *Oh, please, baby, just be quiet for a few minutes. Your papa will be back soon, I promise.*

"Mary! Come here!"

Her daughter appeared next to the sofa.

"Take the baby and see if you can calm him down." She handed Abel to Mary, who cradled him in her small arms. "Just sing to him."

"All right, mama. We're out of water."

"I'll get some more," Helen said, thankful for a chance to get away from them all, even if it meant going down into the cellar. *I just need a few minutes. A few minutes to myself.* "You watch your brothers and sister now."

"Yes, mama."

Helen removed the chair in front of the cellar door and went downstairs, a candle in her right hand. The cellar was cooler than upstairs, but not by much. When she got to the bottom of the stairs, Helen held the candle out before her so she could see better. The tiny flame created dancing shadows as its meager light passed over each corner of the cellar. She set the candle down on a small shelf Lucas had installed at the bottom of the stairs just for that purpose. At one end of the room was an improvised clothes line. She'd been forced to hang their clothes in the cellar so they could dry without getting too much dust in them. At the moment, a long, white bed sheet hung from the line.

Helen went to the shelves on the opposite side of the cellar and took down a heavy jug of water. As she did so, her gaze fell on Lucas' shotgun. It was leaning against the wall just below a small wooden shelf with an unopened box of slugs. She hesitated when she saw it, then headed toward the stairs with the water jug. Out of the corner of her eye, she saw the hanging sheet flutter, as though someone hiding behind it had poked it with their fingers. Helen shuddered. *It's a draft. It has to be a draft.* She reached the stairs and picked up the candle, her eyes on the sheet as she went. It flapped at the edges nearest the cellar's dirt floor, more noticeably this time.

"Johnny, are you down here?" *I told that girl to watch them. What's wrong with her today?* "Johnny, is that you?"

Helen put the jug down and went to the sheet. She was about to pull it back when she thought she heard something on the other side. She put her ear up to the sheet to listen. Then, she heard it. Whispering.

"Who's there?" she murmured. "Johnny?"

The whispering got louder, but not loud enough for Helen to make out what was being said. The sheet brushed her ear and she felt someone or something poke her from the other side. Helen shrieked and ran up the stairs, taking the water jug as she went. Back in the kitchen, she slammed the cellar door and put the chair back under the door knob. Several moments passed before she took her eyes off the door. The children were all at the table, regarding her in silence.

"Did one of you go down there?" she asked.

None of them answered.

"I told you to stay out of there! What's *wrong* with you children today?"

Johnny's eyes started to tear up.

"Don't you cry! Don't you *dare* cry!" Helen bellowed at him. The outburst produced the exact opposite effect she'd desired.

"You're scaring us, mama," Mary said from the living room, Abel still in her arms.

Helen fell into the chair in front of the cellar door and covered her face with her hands. *Oh, Lord, what is happening to me?* She started to shake, trying to hold back the tears.

"Mama," Johnny said, "it's all right. We still love you."

Lucille got out of her chair and went to Helen. She placed her tiny hand on her mother's arm. "We'll always love you, mama."

Helen broke down and hugged her daughter tight. "I'll always love you too."

Mary was at her side then. "We're sorry, mama. We didn't mean to be bad. Just don't hurt us anymore."

Helen looked at Mary. "Hurt you? Mary, I could never hurt you."

"We'll be good from now on, promise," Mary said. "We won't make any more noise."

She pulled her close, her arms full of children now. Then, the phone rang. Helen jumped, frightened by the unexpected and long awaited sound of someone from the outside world making contact. She stared at the phone for a moment, not sure what to do, then snapped out of it and rushed across the kitchen to where it sat on the table.

"Hello? Lucas?"

A faint voice, interrupted by loud static, echoed on the other end of the line. "Helen?"

"Lucas? Can you hear me? Oh, God, where are you?" "I'm coming home."

She turned to her children. "Pa's comin' home!" They took the news in silence. "Where are you Lucas?"

"I'm almost home. And I'm coming for you."

His words took all the joy and relief out of her voice. "Coming for me?"

"For what you did."

Helen started to cry again. "I don't understand. I haven't done anything!"

"Yes, you have."

"Lucas, what are you saying? You're scarin' me!"

"Soon, Helen." The menace in his voice was unmistakable now. "I'll be home soon."

The line went dead, filled once again with static.

Helen put the phone down and looked to the children. "That was your pa."

"We know," Mary replied, taking a step toward her mother. The other children followed suit. "He's mad with you, mama. Real mad."

Helen backed away from the kitchen. "You're lying. You're trying to trick me. That's enough of these games!"

Outside, the wind blew hard, making the house creak. Helen went to the window and pulled back the sheet. The day had grown darker, if that was possible. Dust devils swept across the prairie like swirling ghosts, forming then dying, then forming again, interrupted only by the occasional rolling tumbleweed. Then, she saw it. The silhouette of a dark figure walking slowly toward the house. Helen squinted, trying to make out its features, but the dust was too thick. Her heart started to beat fast. Lucas' words, if it had indeed been her husband on the telephone, came back to her. *I'm coming for you, Helen. For what you did.*

"I haven't done anything!" she cried again.

The figure was close now. It wore an old fedora and a long coat, the same ones Lucas wore when he left the house that day. *Is that him? Why doesn't his hat blow off? He's not even holding it.* Helen let the sheet fall back. The wind gusted against the side of the house, knocking the rocking chair on the porch onto its side. The clatter made Helen scream. She looked to the children. They remained standing in the kitchen, not moving a muscle, their eyes on her. Helen locked the door and started to push the sofa in front of it.

"Help me, Mary! There's someone coming!"

"It's pa," Mary said.

"Hurry!"

"No, mama. You can't keep pa out."

"Mary, please," Helen begged, sobbing now.

None of the children moved.

Helen screamed when someone rapped on the door. She managed to block the door with the sofa and retreated into the kitchen. "Into the cellar. Now, children."

The knocking on the door became more forceful.

Helen threw the chair blocking the cellar door aside. "Now, children! Now!"

They stared at her, then at the open door. "Pa wants to come in," Mary said. "That's not your father! Get in the cellar!"

The front door splintered as it gave way, but the sofa kept it from opening more than a crack. A gloved hand appeared inside, trying to force the door open.

Helen ran. Down in the cellar, she fumbled around in the dark. After a few minutes, her hands fell on what she was looking for – Lucas' shotgun. Her eyes adjusted to the dark now, she loaded the two barrels and snapped the shotgun closed. Upstairs, the intruder continued to crash against the door. Helen went for the stairs, stopping short when she heard the whispering from behind the white sheet again.

"Who's there?" She placed the stock of the shotgun against the inside of her shoulder. "I said who's there!"

A soft voice on the other side of the sheet called out. "Mama, it's us."

"Mary?"

Upstairs, the front door finally crashed open. Helen heard heavy footsteps across the wooden floors.

Again, Mary called out, "Mama?"

Helen threw the sheet aside and gasped. Her hand went to her mouth and she staggered back. Stacked neatly side by side were her children, their hair and clothes still wet from the baths she'd given them earlier that day. Baby Abel was in Mary's arms. They looked like they were asleep. Helen fell against the wall, her mouth gaping at the sight of her children. The floodgates of memory opened with full force then, filling her mind with that morning's events. A bath for each child, and then sleep. She'd started with Mary. She was the oldest and biggest and put up the toughest fight. Helen's blue eyes were pale and cold as she held Mary under. When she was done, she went for Johnny. He'd hidden under the bed with Lucille. They went easily. Finally, she went into the nursery. Abel was asleep when Helen put him in the tub. It took less than a minute for him to drown. Moving them to the cellar one by one was easy. They were all so small, even Mary, and did not weigh much. The footsteps at the top of the stairs brought Helen back to the present. She reached for the shotgun as a booted foot fell on the top step. The intruder took his time coming down the stairs. At last, his face came into view.

"I've come home, woman," Lucas said as he took off his hat. She lifted the shotgun and rested her chin on the end of the twin barrels. "It was the dust storm," she said, giving her children one final glance. "It was the dust storm that took them. It took us all."

The End.

The Reverend Gets Stuck in a Hole

Glenn Rolfe

Physician: Dr. Peterson
S268-WCT29

Reverend Emmitt Charles stood– quiet, watching, and waiting. So much young flesh, so many innocent minds. He had arrived in town shortly after this morning's glorious sunrise, and was granted an opportunity by the local Pastor, John Clarke, to give a guest sermon to the small town's limited, but beautiful and attentive congregation. He had of course slipped away immediately after finishing his fiery delivery of the Lords word, in dire need of his trusty flask and its red devil brew; a dark gift from a secret friend back in the place he called home.

Pastor Clarke had been kind enough, foolish enough, to invite him to the congregation's Sunday night social gathering. After eyeballing a number of young beauties in the local chapter's stable, there wasn't a chance in hell he would pass up such an ample opportunity.

His sharp brown eyes had tagged his first angel of the evening. She had long golden locks that hung down to the center of her back, a bountiful bosom, and hips to match– just the way he liked them. Her hair had been pulled up in a bun during the day's earlier service, giving way to her most modest look, but here, with the darkness settling over the glassed windows of the large barn located just behind the small church, she had let those delicious golden strands loose. He was damn near salivating at what their future held. The poor sweet thing had no idea what kind of wolf this house of God had let in.

"You have a very nice covenant here. Where's your man?" he asked, his eyes drizzling over the shapes hidden beneath her smock.

"Hello, Sir. Thank you for that powerful sermon earlier. I didn't catch where you were from," she said.

He noticed the ease at which she side stepped his inquiry. "I'm from the north, cold country. May I have the pleasure of knowing your name, madam?"

He watched her pretty green eyes glance over his shoulder, searching the increasingly growing crowd behind him before whispering.

"Anna. Ann Louise Clarke. And you have awfully adventurous eyes for man of God."

Aw, the preacher's daughter.

"You'll have to excuse my–" he paused, stepping back to look her over again, "–wandering gaze. These are the eyes of a man, God fearing or not, and you are a heavenly sight to behold, if and you don't mind my saying, Ms. Clarke."

His charm had never failed him. He watched as the rosy glow blossomed to life over her full, flush cheeks.

"Pastor," she began, fanning at her face with one of her delicate hands.

"–Reverend" he sternly corrected her, with a little more menace in his delivery than he had intended.

He noticed the flash of fear roll across her beautiful features like the rolling grey clouds just before a thunderstorm.

"It's Reverend Charles," he managed. Much more controlled, and much more gentle.

"Sorry if I offended thee, Reverend," she offered." I aimed no intention toward doing so."

"Well, Ms. Clarke, I'm not so easily offended, and you did not even come close to doing so, but if you do feel the need to make up for a misunderstanding, I would gladly accept your apology by way of a dance." He held out his right hand to her.

She took hold of his hand, rosy red all over again, and allowed him to guide her over to join the rest of those who were moving to the white haired piano player's rendition of the hymn, "God Will Take Care of You".

They danced through to the songs end, Reverend Charles looking upon Anna Louise as if she were his Last Supper. The voice inside, a voice he trusted in times such as these, told him that she, while not as obvious in her desires, felt a throbbing within her that he dare think she had not felt for another man in her short lifetime.

The longing she was failing to hide shown like the brightest star in God's great sky. He saw her trying to shake the truth from her undoubtedly fogged mind. She tried to pull away from him.

"I'm sorry, Reverend Charles, but you'll have to excuse me–" He clasped her hand with his own, the strength of his passion adding a sense of urgency to the moment.

"Come with me," he stated, bluntly. He pulled her back to him, eyes alive with something burning hotter than love.

"W-where? Where shall we go?" she said.

"Just around back," he answered. "There's something I'd like to show you."

"Well, I suppose we could slip away," she said. Glancing over his shoulder again, she searched the room. "Let me go out first, so as we're not seen leaving together."

"As you wish, Ms. Clarke," he bowed his head to her, never removing his gaze from her own.

"Out behind the barn, there is a large Sugar Maple on the corner."

"I'll meet you there in three minutes," he said as he parted ways with her, crossing the crowded room for the table of refreshments. He watched from beside the pitcher of lemonade as she fiddled nervously with her hair, and scampered away, silent and sly as a mouse. He could barely contain the excitement coursing through his loins.

"Pardon, Reverend," said an elderly man of the brood.

The Reverend quickly put his game face back in place. "Yes, dear sir."

"I just wanted to let you know, I thought what you preached today was a gift given to us by the Lawd hisself, and I wanted to say thank you." The old man shook the reverend's hand brimming with adoration from ear to ear.

"You said it yourself, Mr...."

"Gilbert, Horace Gilbert, Sir."

"You said it yourself, Mr. Gilbert- 'twas the Lord's work, not mine. So praise be to Him. I am merely a vessel. I'm afraid you'll have to pardon me, Mr. Gilbert. I must use the little boy's room." He gave the old man a strong final shake and an all too perfect smile, before making his escape.

Over his shoulder he heard Horace Gilbert call out, "Thanks all the same, Reverend."

***

The blood of Ms. Anna Louis Clarke, still smeared across his face and hands, showed the Reverend in the light of his truest self– a murdering gentleman. He swigged his fiery brew from the flask as he walked swiftly through the field and away from the church, away from his latest sacrifice. It would be some time before they found the pastor's daughter's body. By then, he would be gone. Besides, who would dare suspect a preacher of such horrors? Surely they would be on the lookout for a couple of Negro scoundrels.

Beyond the field, lay a thin patch of trees. On the other side, he found a dirt road that led toward the next town over. After what seemed like hours of walking east, the Reverend came upon a weathered and warn house. He stepped up onto the porch; the faded and scuffed boards of the steps threatened to give way beneath his boots. Devoid of light, he moved toward the front door, trying the cold metal handle, a sound to his left caught his attention. His eyes darted in the direction of the soft noise, a muffled thud. A second thud followed from his right, then, two more. His eyes slowly acclimated to the near-blackness of the roofed-in porch, two sets of eyes stared back at him from their perch to his left. He turned his head to find two more sets on his right. Cats– filthy, vile creatures– surrounded him. The hair on the back of his neck blossomed to life the way Ms. Anna Louse Clarke's had as he produced his straight razor a few hours ago. Angered by his own weakness, he took three quick steps toward the creatures to his left. On the third step, the brittle board beneath his boot gave way. His leg disappeared up to the knee. He cried out as the sinking joint drove into the broken pieces of wood; he felt blood from the fresh wound dripping down his shin.

The eyes stared back at him. The creatures they belonged to had not so much as flinched at his foolish attempt to intimidate them. And, as if by some sort of sorcery, the felines had multiplied three fold. There were a dozen sets of eyes gazing at him as he tried to pull his trapped limb free from the fragile floor.

The night's silence was broken by a low, guttural growl. One was joined by many. In stereo, the creatures, who alone may have been worthy of passing off, took on a terrifying menace, the likes of which the Reverend was used to exuding, not succumbing to. But the fear, ripping up through his vulnerable form, was undeniable. Try as he might, and he did try, the ensnared leg refused to come free. He could feel the blood from his injured knee wetting his sock.

Something beneath the haggard boards nudged his hanging foot. He jerked his boot away, feeling it bump against something else. He let out a howl as needle sharp claws hooked into the exposed flesh of his calf above the top of his boot.

The night around him filled with the howls of the creatures from hell that matched, and then drowned out, his own. The small dark forms surrounded him, stalking him like a pack of tiny wolves in the night.

Through tears, and with a voice quivering like a girl in the face of her defiler, the Reverend cried, "Git back! Git back ye devils. I am your master."

His impotent exclamations were met with more blood curdling shrieks; shrill and stabbing.

The Reverend's false confidence withered, replaced by the whimpers and pleadings of a man about to be hung for his wrongs. And those wrongs began to fill and flood his terrified mind; the Hewitt girl from last summer– a breathtaking girl, 15 years of age– her teeth were still in a small wooden box back at his cabin in Maine; the lovely, but blessedly ignorant Martha Francis of Massachusetts– widow of former Massachusetts, Governor Chauncey Francis– her screams had filled his daydreams, and fueled his desire for the sacrifices like no other had before tonight; and the angel of perfection, Ms. Anna Louise Clarke. There had been countless others since his dark friend had chosen him for these missions.

Being an apostle for the most powerful force under heaven had given him purpose, direction, and something to live, and kill, for. And yet, somehow, he now found himself in this horrible predicament. Were his services no longer needed? Had he fulfilled his Masters wishes? His mission, complete?

"No, no, no, no. G-g-git! Git away...I- I have s-so much more to do, Master..."

The first claw, swung from the closest of the swarming brigade of felines–one with fur as pure as snow– caught the corner of his right eye, tearing the flesh and sending a spray of blood to the decaying grey planks before him. Another from a fat, orange Tabby, caught the side of his nostril and ripped the flesh it snared free. Another razor claw stuck in his brow and sending a flood of crimson into the eye below– he could no longer keep track of his attackers. The next two strikes tore through the pallet of his upper lip, straight through to his gums. The next, dug in across his scalp, just above his left temple. In seconds, his face became a mask of torn flesh and blood. The cat screams– a mix of bestial growls and shrieking mews– filled the reverend's dying, panic-stricken mind. The sins of his past, streaking by his conscience, devoured chunk after chunk of his self-righteous, self-justified, self-satisfying and ungodly ways. Every pound of fear he had ever imposed returned to his shrinking, shriveling id.

As he tried to close his eyes and shut out the barrage of claws and tiny pin-pricking teeth, a sharp nail hooked into the center of his left eye, slicing in and pulling through the soft sclera, taking the gift of sight with it. Before he could comprehend, or defend the loss, another hellcat followed suit clawing and ruining his remaining eye. The reverend's soul-breaking screams pierced the blackened night, becoming the lone audible sound in the dark.

He screamed again, and again, until his wails turned to mumbled ramblings. His torn up body, filled with gashes that varied in their levels of depth and severity, seeping blood onto the dying timber that he remained trapped within. Before long, his mumbling turned to sobs. Blind eyes that burned like hell's most intense inferno, hung–torn and useless– in shreds from sockets of blood. A cold realization began to creep toward his consciousness– he was alone. His Master had abandoned him. There was nothing but the soft breeze, on this chilled evening, sweeping past his tattered and crimson covered ears.

The flock of hellfire felines had vanished as quickly as they had gathered. He had been punished by his dark lord. In a sick twist of fate, he had suffered the cuts, the slashes, the mutilation of his shrine, and the theft of his ability to walk his desired path.

They could have finished me. They should have finished me.

Whether from the emotional catastrophe or from the loss of blood, the Reverend slipped into a quiet and peaceful slumber.

***

"Oh goodness, oh Lawd, Reverend, Oh Lawd is that you?" The Reverend opened his eyes, but saw nothing. He could feel the sun's warmth glazing over his body, sweat breaking out over his exposed forearms and brow, but he was left in total blackness. Then, the pain, the burning, the aches all began to register. And the memory of last night's impossible act of retribution upon his wicked soul, railroaded back to him.

"Reverend, it's me. It's Horace Gilbert, Sir. From Pastor Clarke's church? Lawd, Reverend. We needs to git you help. Aw, this is jest despicable. First Mizz Clarke, an' then you, a man of God."

The Reverend was nauseous at the cruel hand he had been dealt by the one he thought he had so proudly served. And to further the slap in his face, this poor, ignorant Negro man of the pathetic congregation he had just duped, was rescuing him. The Reverend recoiled at the thought.

He felt the gentle nudge and tickle of fur against is ravaged calf below the porch. He swallowed the scream that begged to be freed. Tears stung the congealing wounds around his eye sockets as his thoughts smashed full on into the thick fortress of his skull. In his mind, he saw the sea of cat eyes reappear.

"Reverend, are you still with me?" Horace Gilbert's voice was somewhere off in the background.

Terror displaced all other thoughts, as the murderous gentleman, who had christened himself the Reverend of Tender Flesh, slipped back into the darkness of his dizzying mind.

The End.

Cast Out

John Dennehy

Physician: Dr. Peterson
6268-WCT29

Terrence returned to the shabby motel early evening exhausted. It was more of a grim makeshift dwelling for itinerate workers than a motel, sagging slightly with a rickety balcony that overlooked a decrepit parking lot. The siding was asbestos, a permanent dark blue.

He pulled his antique BMW to the side of the parking area, hoping to avoid dents from drunks. Once the lot had been paved but now it was a mixture of asphalt, chunks of tar, and dirt. Mostly it was dirt.

He quickly ascended the stairwell leading to the second floor. Terrance stood a lean six feet tall and wore a dirty t-shirt, jeans and work boots. His brown hair was artsy long. The building trim and handrail were painted white but were faded and flaky. While climbing the stairs, he hadn't bothered with the handrail.

There were a few old chairs on the balcony. Some had long ago been pulled from rooms and were musty. Terrance saw old Harold squished in a chair. A saxophone lay on the deck beside him and a sheaf of music rest on his portly abdomen.

"How you doing?" Harold said from his tattered chair. He was nearly blind. So his dark eyes only looked generally in Terrance's direction.

"Good," Terrance replied. "How about yourself?"

Harold smiled kindly. "Been better," he said. "But I'm doing okay."

"Didn't clean up down at the intersection today, huh?" "Nope," Harold said grinning. "People just don't appreciate fine jazz nowadays."

"I'm not so sure about that."

"Well, not enough to make a contribution," Harold said. "If you know what I mean."

Terrance nodded. But Harold's eyes didn't seem to follow. "I guess not," Terrance agreed. "But this might not be the city for it either."

"It's not New York for sure."

"I was thinking Memphis," Terrance said. "Memphis would be better business."

Harold nodded. "Sure, sure would," Harold complied. "But how am I going to get there. You going to drive me?"

"You have a point."

"Sure do."

"Well, maybe you could think about downtown," Terrance offered. "More people are inclined to stop and pay tribute on a sidewalk than an intersection."

Harold laughed and slapped his leg. "Pay tribute," he repeated. "That's why I like you boy." He smiled. "Pay tribute," he said again, shaking his head slightly.

"I'm just saying…"

"No, I hear you," Harold said. "I'm not complaining. Doing just fine right here. Greensboro is just fine. But I could of done a little better today."

Terrance reached into his pocket. He pulled out a couple of dollars and tossed them into the saxophone case.

"Mighty obliged."

"No problem."

Just as Terrance began to step by, Harold grabbed his hand. It was a surprisingly strong grip for an old man, a beggar musician. Terrance was taken aback. He looked at Harold's vacuous eyes. A vapid eye seemed to bead in on him, while the other peered off in the distance, both were empty and cold.

"What?" Terrance asked trying to wiggle his hand free.

"Listen," Harold said.

"Okay," Terrance said alarmed. "Just let go of me."

"Listen," Harold said more sternly. Pulling Terrance toward him, squeezing his hand like a vice. Harold's eyes seemed to come into focus. Black as coal.

"Okay," Terrance said frightened. "I'm listening." "I helped you get in here, right." "You sure did," Terrance replied.

"And I got you the same price as me."

"Thank you for that," Terrance said nervously.

"Now, I been noticing you been bringing bottles into your room… stuff like that…"

Terrance looked at him quizzically, wondering where this was headed.

"I want you to make a <u>Deal</u> with me," Harold said. By this time Terrance was tethered by his own arm and hunched over, looking eye to eye with the mysterious old man.

"What kind of deal?"

"Look, you're going to cut out of here at some point."

"And?"

"And I want you to promise me that anything you leave <u>behind,</u> is mine."

Terrance relaxed a bit. "Doubt that I'll leave anything, seeing that I don't have much," Terrance said. "But anything left behind is yours."

"I mean _anything_," Harold said clenching his teeth as the last word came out.

"Sure."

"Promise?" Harold insisted.

"I promise," Terrance said. "I have to go now."

"Sure, sure," Harold said turning kind. He patted Terrance's hand and let loose his grip. "You run along now."

***

Terrance woke groggily. The mattress was too soft, cheap and old. He sat up and dangled his legs over the edge of the bed, thinking just another month and he'd move on. There was a pack of Marlboros on the nightstand with a Bic lighter. He grabbed them. And then he pulled on a t-shirt, hanging halfway down his boxers.

He walked into the kitchen, bones aching. His muscles felt fatigued from months of construction work. His head swirled from the bottle of Jack Daniels that had helped him get to sleep.

Sliding a cigarette into his mouth, he flicked a lighter and thought about the agony of facing another day in the hot sun. He had relished the release from papers and grades at first. But now going to the jobsite was worse than going to class. At least in college he could sleep in. You had to listen to the professors and their platitudes. But it was air conditioned and no heavy lifting.

He took a long drag and reached for the coffee pot. Looking it over briefly, he didn't feel like making any. Terrance poured a small bowl of cereal to settle his stomach. Then he slid on his jeans and work boots and stepped outside. The balcony was quiet except for a woman leaving the unit at the end. Harold's chair was empty. The saxophone was nowhere to be seen.

Terrance descended the stairwell and got into his BMW. He drove to a nearby Crispy Cream for coffee. Bought two and then quickly headed over to an apartment complex and picked up a married worker, Rick.

Rick sat slouching with the coffee cup perched against his pot belly. "This car is immaculate," Rick said looking it over.

"Thanks," Terrance said flatly, trying to brush it off.

"How did you come by it?"

"Uh," Terrance mused, "got it a while back." Rick glanced at him skeptically.

"How are you doing?" Terrance said after an awkward moment. "Well, you know," Rick said. "Morning comes early." They both grinned.

"Sure does."

"So, why are you even working construction?" "Same as you," Terrance offered. "Need the money." "Naw, I'm saying… a smart kid like you could be doing something more," Rick said. "You know, work in an office." "They don't hire dropouts," Terrance responded. And then he turned up the volume on the stereo and the discussion fell off.

Terrance whipped the car around the last tight turn leading to the jobsite. Clenching a handgrip on the door, Rick failed to conceal his fright of the intense speed. As the car's stereo blared, Terrance could feel power from the speeding car and loud music; it raced through his veins. Pushing the car to its limits made him feel like he had some control in his life.

He pulled the car over to the side of the road near a lot where a house was being built. Most of the other workers had just pulled through ruts into the work area. But they either drove jalopies or heavy duty trucks.

Rick and Terrance piled out of the car and strolled over to the work site. Having a pot belly and stubby legs caused Rick to drop a few paces behind. They were late. Everyone else had already tossed their coffee cups and begun working.

Terrance saw Gerald the foreman glaring their way.

"Good evening ladies!" Gerald barked at them.

They stretched it out and Rick fell even further behind.

As they picked up the pace to a slow trot, workers jeered at them through windows and open beams. Some nodded in appreciation. Terrence suspected they had heard the screeching of his tires.

Splitting up, Rick headed for a trench that he was digging on the far side of the house. Terrence went around back and climbed up a rickety ladder, a makeshift device serving as the rear steps. He went into the room framed for the kitchen, and walked over to the spot where he left his tool belt. It was gone.

At first he thought someone had filched it. But then he realized that Bobby Lynn was getting some payback. Terrance looked around for him. Typically, he was easy to spot because of his emaciated body from smoking too much reefer. He expected to see Bobby Lynn's slender mug pop between two studs with a wide grin showing his crooked, yellowed teeth.

But Bobby Lynn wasn't anywhere in sight.

Terrence thought for a bit. Then he went out back and began climbing a ladder to the roof.

His thighs ached. So he climbed the ladder slowly. Terrance glanced over at his car and remembered getting it as a present for graduating prep school in New Hampshire. The brittle rungs from the ladder chaffed at his hands. He thought about how things went wrong. Beginning with the girl. Then dropping out of Duke.

When he reached the roof, Terrence didn't notice that the shingles were damp. Lost in thought. Thinking of how his blue blazer was exchanged for a grubby t-shirt. The striped tie traded for a tool belt, and stone chinos for jeans. Penny loafers switched to work boots. He saw his tool belt perched on top of the chimney, and started up the steep hip roof. One hand holding the soffit trim of a dormer.

His eyes were focused on the tool belt, and his mind was thinking of the girl, when his feet began to slide. Terrance began slipping downward fast. He churned his feet. At the edge of the roof, he was essentially running in place. Still having a hand on the soffit, he pulled hard while the other grasped at the roof finding only air.

Suddenly there was traction and he began to ascend the roof. He saw a few guys looking up at him, their mouths agape.

"His feet spun around like a cartoon character," one said.

"He grew claws," another added.

Terrance didn't pay them any mind. He was unfazed about almost tumbling two stories below. Terrance continued upward. He knew the other guys saw him differently. Most were high school dropouts; he had dropped out of a national college, and it wasn't because of his grades. Then he slipped again.

Sliding down the roof was accompanied by the eerie dispatch of grit breaking loose from the shingles. He dropped to the roof deck and skidded a little further. Then he got up and slowly ascended the roof ridge.

As Terrance carefully treaded across the ridge he thought about his peers. He had worked hard to gain their respect. At first he'd drawn a lot of flack. He had been limber. But the work toned up his muscles the same as it did theirs. Terrance learned to stifle their sarcastic remarks with his wit. He had also learned that they had an appreciation for hard drinking, hard work, and his reckless driving.

Leaning against the chimney gave him a bird's-eye view of the site. He put on his tool belt. The early June morning had begun sunny and bright, but in typical North Carolina fashion, dark clouds moved in fast and unexpectedly. Then there was a clap of thunder.

A few sprinkles began to fall, quickly dampening the work area. Looking down from the highest peak, Terrance felt melancholy hanging overhead with the dark clouds. Below, the workers hurried around grabbing sheets of plastic. They covered the lumber and prepared for the storm. Most had a skip in their step. They had worked enough long days to get a full week's pay so knocking off early on a Friday was welcomed. They moved about like worker ants scurrying around in joy. But Terrance was not included; he'd rather put in the time.

He looked down at the quickly soaking soil. And then he scanned the little piles of construction debris scattered about the site. There were plastic soda bottles and foam fast-food containers mixed with strips of tar paper and bits of sheet rock; the bulk of the piles were discarded waste of lumber and siding. A few domestic beer cans made it into the heaps. Terrance also noticed cigarette butts strewn about.

The lumber being stacked and covered was the only benevolent thing below. With neatly cut edges and the concern that it was always afforded, the lumber brought him a pleasant feeling. Reminded by the scent of freshly sawed lumber, he breathed in heavily. Terrance could feel the humid air in his lungs.

The pinnacle of the scene below was the kiosk in the corner of the lot. Terrance avoided using it at all costs. He marveled at how some workers could use the dank little chamber like they were at home. And others went in there to get some help through the day.

The rain got stronger and began to soak his t-shirt. Workers below began to wrap things up more quickly, paying less attention to detail. Then he carefully made his descent to the worksite below.

The lumber was covered and the tools put away. Gerald handed out paychecks in the framed-in garage, and then everybody scurried through the drizzling rain to their vehicles. Rick plodded off with another married worker. By the time Terrance reached his car on the street everyone was gone. Some had pealed out in joy totally disregarding the slippery roads.

***

He turned over his ignition and the old BMW sputtered, so he pumped the gas pedal and tried it again. This time the engine roared to life. He let the car idle for a moment and turned on the stereo and windshield wipers.

Terrance slowly pulled onto the road. He executed a perfect three point turn. Then he headed back down the same road taken earlier. Only now he poked along instead of speeding recklessly.

He took his time going home. Mainly because the dingy motel room was desolate. Other guys had reason to race home. Some had families. The rest were kicking up the weekend partying early.

As Terrance drove, the rain broke into a heavy downpour. A cloud of melancholy slipped over him. He felt despair. While the rain pelted the windshield, and the wipers squeaked back and forth, everything seemed hazy. He felt as though he was in a dream; it seemed like he was just coasting down the road. Nothing appeared real. A chimerical trip.

The car seemed to be driving itself. Entering the city, it felt like the little BMW was starting and stopping at red lights on its own. Terrance was functioning on reflex; no conscious thoughts of his own. He felt in a void, distinct from the rest of the world.

Even though everything seemed unreal, Terrance knew that if he swung the wheel hard, the car would swerve into a brick building. The sheet metal would crunch and bricks would pop loose. His front end would cave in. There would be broken bones jaggedly piercing his skin, torn through his jeans. Blood would spatter about the compartment. And the pain would most definitely be excruciating. The dream would end; his bubble burst.

This macabre image caused him to ponder a dark reality. If he died, nobody would care.

Stopped at a light, his despair slipped away momentarily. He gazed over at some girls in a Honda. One of them slipped out her tongue, glided it around her lips, and then blew him a kiss. For an instant his concerns seemed far away. He flashed an approving grin. The uplift made his surroundings seem real again.

Soon Terrance was tapping his fingers on the steering wheel to the beat of music. The dark cloud of his despair ebbed. The rain let up and the car rolled along.

As he turned into the motel parking lot, Terrance realized that he hadn't lost the dark cloud. Despair loomed above the motel. It was lingering there, waiting for him. The dingy motel seemed to mock him.

He turned off the ignition. The image of the filthy construction site came to mind. For a moment, he pondered about his working conditions compared to people who finish college. Despair entangled him.

Terrance opened the door. The rain had stopped but the ground was saturated. It was humid and getting warmer quickly as the sun poked through clouds. Flipping the driver's seat forward, he reached into the back for a large, black duffle bag. Terrance hauled it off the seat and threw it over his shoulder. He locked the car and headed for the stairs.

His few valuables were packed in the duffle bag. Terrance typically brought the bag to his room at night, except when he was too tired or drunk to bother with it. Most days he lugged it to the car, leaving it in the trunk or on the backseat while he worked. When he reached the balcony, Terrance felt slightly lightheaded.

He slowly walked along the porch. The edges were wet. But most of it remained dry, protected by the building. As he expected, the rain had driven Harold from his post at the intersection. He lay in a chair fast asleep. The saxophone was in its case on the plank flooring nearby.

Terrance quietly stepped past while reaching for his keys. He opened the door and felt cool air permeate from the passageway. It smelled moldy. Stepping inside, Terrance cut on the light and walked across the room. He heaved his bag onto the bed, and then he went over to the small kitchen area and fished around for a glass in the cupboard. There was a bottle of whiskey on the counter. Although it wasn't even noon, he poured half a glass, and then took a seat by the window.

Occasionally, on days like this, he would sit on the balcony and listen to Harold's yarns. But today he preferred solitude after the odd exchange the night before. Terrance peered out the window and saw Harold still slouched in the chair. His belly rose and fell peacefully in a tranquil stupor. A wisp of smoke appeared to be meandering above Harold.

Terrance set his glass on the windowsill. Then he stepped onto the balcony to check it out. The faint stream of smoke seemed to hover over Harold's belly, causing Terrance concern that a cigarette might be burning.

He approached. As he got closer, the smoke seemed less discernible; but he hadn't observed it dissipate. Alongside Harold, he couldn't see any smoke at all, so he looked around. No cigarette butt burning on the deck. Nothing.

He went back to the room. Terrance gulped down the whiskey and then lit a cigarette. He took a few drags and looked out at Harold. The smoke was back.

He stepped out. Standing next to Harold the only smoke in sight stemmed from the butt in Terrance's mouth. He looked around again. But there was nothing. As he went back to his room, Terrance peered over his shoulder. No smoke. He went inside and poured another glass and drank it greedily, then sat down with a cigarette.

While he nursed another whiskey, his mind came back to the girl. She was an attractive sister of a prep school friend. At the time, he had been seventeen and she was much younger, but seemed experienced.

Turning to the window, he saw the smoke again. He tried to ignore it this time. His thoughts stuck on the girl. Blonde with blue eyes. He realized her lack of experience immediately. She hadn't handled it well.

The trail of smoke lingered over Harold. Terrance stepped out again. Standing by the old man the smoke was gone, so he kneeled and closely inspected beneath the chair and surrounding deck. Again there was nothing. He went downstairs to see if it was emanating from below. But he didn't find anything.

Partway up the stairs, he saw the smoke clearly. Terrance gazed with his head only slightly higher than the balcony deck. It was a wisp hovering over the old man extending two feet high and about five inches wide at the thickest point. The smoke did not emanate from the balcony floor. But somehow it seemed to exude from Harold's belly.

He walked over. Harold was sound asleep and the smoke was gone. Terrance looked him over carefully. Harold's shirt was pulled tight around his large belly. It was puzzling. There was no sign of the source so he did a hasty scan and didn't see anyone. Then he reached between two buttons of Harold's shirt. Grasping around inside the shirt, he found no purchase. Terrance shook his head at the baffling phantasm.

Harold stirred and muttered, "Hey, what's going on?" Terrance stepped back.

Harold sat up. He was clearly disoriented, looking this way and that trying to discern what was happening with poor sight.

"It's okay," Terrance said trying to assuage him. "I was just checking on you."

"Checking on me for what, son?" Harold said. "I got about fifty cent before the rain set in. Not much to pilfer."

"No, I wasn't trying to take your money," Terrance said.

"I expect not," Harold replied sitting up. "Cause you know I'll knock you into next week."

"Sure do."

"So what's going on?" Harold said raising an eyebrow.

"I thought that I saw some smoke out here," Terrance said, "like a cigarette butt burning. But I looked around and couldn't find anything."

Harold betrayed a knowing grin.

"What?"

Harold shrugged. "What are you worried about?"

"I was concerned that the source of the smoke could cause a fire," Terrance offered. "Like something could ignite and burn the place down."

Harold leaned back and grinned. He nodded his head in understanding. "Son, you don't have to worry about a fire. Nothing here is burning."

"What is it then?"

"How should I know," Harold replied turning his hands up confounded. "Just know nothing been burning out here. So there ain't nothing to worry about. Must be the humid air."

Terrance didn't buy the reason. But he had no explanation for it either.

Harold nodded. "If you don't mind," he said. Then he slouched back into his chair and closed his eyes. Before they shut, the eyes momentarily appeared like pieces of coal.

"Sure," Terrance said and slinked away.

***

Inside his room, Terrance closed the drapes and focused on the bottle. The hours ticked by slowly. He eventually passed out slumped in the chair. Later he startled awake with the vision of black eyes imprinted upon his mind. A bead of sweat ran down his face despite the air conditioning. He reached for his forehead with the back of a hand; his hairline was saturated with sweat. As he began to sit upright, Terrance felt dizzy. His equilibrium was off, disoriented.

He leaned back and looked around. The whiskey bottle was strewn on its side, empty. He had a smoke. Then he started to do what he'd begun many times, but never went through with it. Fear of what lay beyond always stopped him.

He walked to the bed feeling muddled. Terrance grabbed the duffle bag, slid it over, and unzipped the main compartment. Reaching in deep, he fished around and grabbed hold of his 9mm Glock.

Terrance calmly walked to the bathroom. He felt numb. His body was limber and everything was surreal. The walls and fixtures seemed blurry and indistinct. The pistol in his hand was the only thing with weight.

He stepped into the tub. Then he glanced at the mildewed tile and the scum around the drain. Sitting down he clicked off the safety and brooded over his misgivings: the girl, dropping out of college, always disappointing his parents. He was alone.

He raised the pistol, opened his mouth and slid the barrel in. The metal was cold and the weapon felt awkward, clanking his teeth.

Terrance closed his eyes. A bead of sweat ran down his forehead. He took a deep breath. The despair that consumed him seemed to entangle his lungs, so he breathed heavily again. The air was thick and heavy. His numbness was a buffer to fear.

Then he slowly squeezed the trigger.

Within milliseconds of firing, he glimpsed the wisp of smoke. It was wafting toward him bringing along a terrible stench; the decay of flesh rotting over the eons.

His body slammed back into the tub. Then fissures ripped down his arms, along his sides, and through his legs. The pain was extreme. Terrance screamed out in agony. His skin was husked back, the exposed meat crimson. Blood from the flesh dripped and ran into the tub. An indiscernible peeling ensued as his body lay in the tub.

There were no more lacerations to the flesh. But he felt the terror of being shucked from his meat sack. Terrance discerned the culling of his soul from its corporal body. The anguish shot through him pricking into every nerve ending, pulsating extreme torment into every aspect of his being. The scourge reverberated and magnified his pain. He wanted to black out but couldn't.

And then the suffering subsided.

He was hovering above his discarded body, looking down upon it. The wisp of smoke moved closer with two coal black eyes peeking from the fogginess. Watching in horror as it settled beneath his skin. Then the blood in the tub ran back to the flesh. The fissures closed. There were no marks upon the body.

Then he noticed the chunks of grey matter on the tile above his head. It was splattered along with bits of bone and thick, dark blood. The grey matter trembled and then slid beneath his artsy hair. Followed by the bits of bone. Dense beads of blood formed then ran toward the artsy long hair and disappeared beneath it.

Hovering above, he was aghast to see his body sit upright. It was completely intact. Then Terrance heard his own voice, "Whatever you leave behind is mine," the resurrected said. The eyes appeared dark as coal for a moment.

Then Terrance went into black.

The End.

The Dark Side

Lex Sinclair

Physician: Dr. Peterson
S268-WCT29

Andy Meyers was only twenty-five years-old when he died of a massive heart attack. The rumour floating around the small town was he had seen something terrible that had induced a tremendous, unexpected shock. His heart ceased beating abruptly. Nobody knew what the shock was that ended Andy's life so suddenly... in such bizarre circumstances. In any small town news gets around. Especially bad, inexplicable news.

James, the town's gravedigger, sat a good distance from the hole in the ground, awaiting the arrival of the hearse. Already the cemetery grounds were crowded with mourners dressed in their funeral attire. Close friends, work colleagues and acquaintances who knew Andy stood close together wearing sombre expressions - near his grave – talking in hushed voices.

Whenever someone young and affable died there was always a big turnout. Today was no exception. James knew Andy well. James was a gravedigger fifteen years ago when Andy had been baptised in St. John's church, situated at the other end of the cemetery. Andy had everything someone his age could ask for – good-looks, well-educated, and very popular with the townsfolk. The girls' who Andy knew, fancied him; the boys envied his charisma... and now it was all gone, wiped out in a blink of an eye with nothing but a hazy memory left behind.

The hearse slowed to a halt on the concrete path, and Andy's coffin was carried out by grieving bearers towards the vacant hole. James tried to keep out of sight during the burial services. The last thing a mourner wanted to see was the gravedigger waiting for the service to end so that he could start refilling the hole. Nevertheless, Andy had been a friend of his, too, just like he had been a friend to everyone else attending the service today. James shed a tear for the boy, but nothing compared to the grief that the boy's mother and the father were going through. He could hear their weeping from where he sat in the shade of an old oak tree.

To outlive your own child must be unbearable, James could only imagine. The reverend finished his passage from the Holy Bible and closed the tome before making a sign of the cross above the coffin. Mourners approached the coffin in a single file and placed a red rose atop the varnished coffin and said their final farewells with tears in their eyes.

Once the service was over, the mourners silently wandered away from the graveside and headed back to their cars. They drove away, leaving James alone in the cemetery with a hole to fill once the coffin had been lowered into the ground. It seemed so deceiving that once the service was over that the world should carry on like nothing had happened. The world had only ended for Andy. James got up from the tree stump where he had been perched and made his way to the grave.

The mahogany coffin was shaded from the dazzling sunlight by the four sides surrounding it. Reluctantly, James started to fill the hole. Half an hour passed by rather quickly, and James's shirt was drenched with sweat and which glued itself to his back. The hole was almost filled when the old man heard a knocking sound. He listened again (not believing what he heard distinctly), and a few seconds later heard a thumping sound coming from the ground below. In a panic, James shovelled the soil back out of the hole recklessly, until he reached the lid of the coffin.

Andy is banging the inside of the lid ferociously.

'Hang on, Andy!' he yelled.

He used his crowbar and lump hammer to break open the coffin. However, the old man was not ready for what he was about too see – the body lying supine in the coffin was Andy's. But when he opened his eyes and looked into James's, the gravedigger instinctively knew that it wasn't Andy: it was an evil presence that had taken over his corpse. It sat upright and pulled itself up to a vertical base. The entity that had taken over Andy's body clambered out of the grave and came after James, staring fixedly into his eyes, causing him to stumble and lose his balance. James gazed up at the darkness looming from behind the eyes, which were not human, staring into his soul.

The entity reached out and touched his face before everything in his vision was consumed by perpetual darkness.

It was dusk when James arrived home and parked the Ford outside. He got out and sauntered up the path to the front door in a daze. His wife Audrey came out of the kitchen to greet him, as he stood in the hall in his dirty overalls.

'You're later than I thought you were going to be. I was getting worried.'

James didn't answer. Instead he just stared at her impassively.

'Are you all right?' Audrey asked.

James nodded before speaking. 'I'm fine. I just need to get cleaned up.'

Audrey watched her husband climb the staircase, looking concerned. Her husband wasn't his usual chatty self. Then she assumed it was probably the shock of having to bury his late friend.

James stood under the warm shower spray with his eyes closed and whistled to a chirpy tune, nonchalantly. When he opened his eyes again they were entirely black and utterly inhuman. There was not a trace of his former personality left.

When he finished in the bathroom and went back downstairs James's eyes appeared to be his own again. He sat down at the kitchen table opposite his wife who smiled politely at him. Audrey poured orange juice from the carton into his glass, and rested it down on the coaster next to the dinner plate containing barbecued flavour chicken and chips.

'Does anyone know yet, what might have caused that boy's heart attack?'

James shook his head.

Audrey shrugged, and then combed her grey tangled hair with her fingers. She could sense that James was not feeling quite himself, which unsettled her being in his presence. Usually he discussed his feelings with her openly. Maybe if she changed the subject that would help, she thought.

'I cooked your favourite. You must be hungry after doing all that digging and refilling the grave?'

James looked down at the plate of food and then back to his wife with no expression. 'Yes. This looks really good. Thank you.'

He watched her pick up her utensils and cut a slice of chicken off the bone, then did the same.

When they had eaten and Audrey washed the plates and cutlery, James got up and left the room. All through their meal Audrey had tried to make light conversation, until finally she gave up with the one word, expressionless answers she was getting from her husband. James was now sitting in the living room watching the television screen when she came into the room and plopped herself down next to him. Minutes passed by before one of them finally broke the uncomfortable silence.

'I want to show you something,' James said in a faraway voice.

'What is it? Show me?' Audrey said, regarding him intently, intrigued.

He turned his body so that he faced her and said, 'My beautiful eyes.'

A piercing scream that would have woken the dead emitted from the back of Audrey's throat at the sight of those ink-black, inhuman eyes, as her husband seized her head in his callused hands and passed the contagion on.

***

In less than a week the whole town's population had been invaded by the body snatchers from another realm. The virus had started with the sudden death of Andy, and had spread throughout the small town unobtrusively, gradually taking over anything human left alive. There were only three humans left in the town, who hid in detached house - Ben, Gemma and Colin.

Ben had been dating Gemma for six months. They'd met and got to know one another in the local school. Ben had fled his home narrowly escaping an unthinkable death at the hands of his own parents two days ago. He'd crashed through his bedroom window and landed on the rear lawn. Injured, from a piece of glass that had embedded itself into his left arm and bleeding, Ben headed straight to his girlfriend's house instead of getting someone to call for an ambulance. Usually, this would be considered a stupid thing to do. However, in these circumstances, hindsight had informed him that doing what he did had saved his life.

He had nowhere else to go when he came to his girlfriend's home explaining to them what had happened. Colin listened without interruption to his detailed story, making certain that this was no hoax, before showing his wife's corpse sprawled out on the mattress in their bedroom, after she too, had attempted to take his and Gemma's life. They too hadn't noticed anything was amiss until it was almost too late.

Now they sat in the living room armed, after locking all the windows, and barred the front and back door shut from the inside. Ben rested the handgun he was holding on the arm of the sofa, exhausted. Colin looked at him pointing the barrel of the shotgun to the floor. 'Did you sleep at all?'

Ben leaned back into the seat. 'No, not really. How 'bout you?'

Colin deliberately ignored the young man's question as he stood up.

105

'What do you think has happened?' Ben asked.

'I dunno. But from what I can gather, the townsfolk have formed some kinda cult, and are killing anyone who won't join their faction.'

Ben glanced at his girlfriend who had fallen to sleep. 'Whadda we gonna do about it?'

Colin didn't answer immediately. Instead he stared out of the window, watching the sun creep over the horizon.

'The only thing we can do is get a car and get outta this town.'

'Don't you think that's a bit of a risk?'

Colin turned away from the window. 'If we stay in here any longer they'll find us and break in. If we're trapped inside, we'll be outnumbered.'

Ben nodded, concurring with his girlfriends' father. Yesterday they had watched through the curtains as a group of the intruders had removed the engine from Colin's car and wrecked the bodywork, before puncturing the tyres for good measure. Ben looked at him now.

'How do you suppose we get a vehicle, without being seen?'

Leaning over the arm of the sofa, Colin whispered, 'I'll have to go and look for one and bring it back here.' He paused, hesitant on what he is about to say next. 'If I don't return, it'll be up to you to protect my daughter. Can I trust you, Ben?'

The young man fought back the urge to let his emotions get the better of him. 'You gotta be sure that this is what you want to do. If it all goes bad out there and you lead them back here we'll be dead before sunset. If you're going, Colin, make sure you get back.'

Now on the road armed with his shotgun, Colin walked along the main street that ran the length of the town. The road was as quiet as a grave. There were no cars driving past or other pedestrians walking on the pavement. Even the shops, with their entrance doors gaping wide open were deserted. There was not a trace of life in the once hectic town. Now a ghost town.

The ex-policeman noticed a white transit van parked outside the local convenience store up on the kerb. Scanning the area for anyone lurking in the dark recesses nearby, he then jogged towards the vehicle and opened the door. Colin was surprised when he found the keys already in the ignition and punched the air in jubilation. 'Yes!' he cried out, reprimanding himself for breaking the deafening silence of the eerie ambience.

He pulled away from the kerb and onto the road back to his house, overjoyed that he was inside the moving van and no longer on foot, vulnerable to attack. He started to relax now that he felt safe and secure, but as he turned left around a sharp corner he saw two men in the rear-view mirror in the back of the van coming for him with the darkness filling their eyes ready to assail him and take control of his body.

'Oh shit!'

The middle–aged man realised what was about to happen, and stamped on the brake pedal. The van's wheels locked and the tyres screeched, burning rubber skid-marks on the road in its wake. One of the men crashed spectacularly through the windscreen, bounced off the bonnet and landed on the ground with a sickening thud.

Colin tried to fight off the other man from the driver's seat, but was overpowered in his incapacitated and limited position. The last thing Colin saw as he fought in vain was the inky black in the eyes that looked like two marbles of the creature seizing his head with its bare hands. He thrashed about manically in one last attempt to either flee or overpower the inhuman assailant

***

Darkness descended on the town. Inside the house Ben and Gemma waited anxiously for Colin's return. Ben peeked through the parted curtains at the street outside, unable to sit still for five minutes without fidgeting.

Gemma, who was now wide awake, stood behind her boyfriend, annoyed with him and her dad.

'Why couldn't we have all gone together?' she complained.

'It would've been too risky. We don't know what state the town is in.'

The young woman buried her head in her hands, sighing.

'If it's so risky, then why did he have to go outside in the first place?'

Ben closed the curtain over. 'If we all stay in here, they'll eventually find us and break in. We'll have nowhere to go once they're inside, don't you see?'

Tears streamed down her face. Ben wiped them away with trembling hands and gently kissed her on the cheek.

'But we're barricaded in, for God's sake!'

'Once they break through the windows they would outnumber us. There's too many of them, and not enough ammunition to kill them all.' Ben put a supportive arm around his girlfriend, pulling her close to him.

'I hope he comes back soon.'

'So do I,' he replied, looking over his shoulder towards the window.

Another hour went by, and there was still no sign of Colin.

Although he did not say anything, Ben's heart – along with his hope - was beginning to sink, and he was starting to believe that something unspeakable had befallen Gemma's father. He would have to make a decision soon - to either stay inside or to face the goings on outside and try to find a vehicle for get them out of town safely. What he dreaded more than anything else, though, was if Colin hadn't made it on his own, armed. What chance did two people with a handgun have? The answer was unthinkable.

Gemma had cried a lot since she had been awake and learned that her father had left the safety of the domain. Unable to cope with her fragile state of mind, Ben got up from the arm of the sofa, left the living room and went upstairs to the bathroom to be alone, so he could reflect. He sat down on the toilet seat and thought about what he was going to do next. The 'others' would be searching the town for the last few remaining humans. It was only a matter of time before they found the two of them in her home. Then what?

The young man went over to the sink and turned the cold water tap on. He splashed his face with water, as he stared at his unrecognisable pallid and haggard reflection in the mirror before drying himself off with the hand towel on the rail.

As he was about to put it back Ben heard Gemma shouting up the stairs. 'Ben! Come quick! He's outside!'

A wave of overwhelming relief and elation flooded him. He bounded down the stairs, holding onto the banister, and followed his girlfriend into the living room. She threw open the curtains and pointed to the white van parked outside the house, where Colin could be seen in the driver's seat, motioning for them to hurry up and get outside.

Ben couldn't help but smile broadly.

In his haste, he grabbed the handgun and pulled on his jacket. Gemma shoved the heavy bookcase - that was leaning up against the door - over and unfastened the locks. Then she opened the door and stepped outside, with her boyfriend in her wake.

Excited, Gemma opened the passenger door and clambered inside and moved across so Ben could get in, too. He slammed the door shut before looking at Colin, grinning, admiringly.

'I thought you weren't gonna make it,' Ben said in awe. Colin reciprocated his smile 'It was a close call,' he said, indicating the shattered windscreen.

Gemma leaned over and hugged her dad, proud of him for finding a vehicle to get them out of the town once and for all.

'Thank God you did,' Ben said.

The van pulled away from the kerb. Gemma hugged and kissed her father again as they approached the main road. This time shedding tears of tremendous joy she'd never experienced until now.

'Is that door closed on your side, Ben?' Colin asked.

Ben tried the handle, which was secure.

'Yeah, it's locked all right.'

The darkness, like black ink, spilled over Colin's eyes as he gazed out the space where the windscreen used to be and wind danced in their hair at the road ahead and grinned malevolently to himself. 'Good.'

The End.

Zombie Apocalypse Now!

Rachel Tsoumbakos

Physician: Dr. Roundtree
8245-AVD12

LAST SESSION

#10

The moans of the undead filled the hall. Tatiana pushed Rosalyn behind herself and waved her crowbar around. Pippa stepped forward, also covering the distraught woman and levelled her gun at the mob of zombies in front of them. Her shaking hands made the gun swing around wildly.

"Walter!" Rosalyn's screams were raw and jagged, similar now in tone to the moans of the hideous creatures they faced. Walter paused every time Rosalyn bellowed. His nose lifted to the air, his mouth open, devouring the scent of his still living wife.

Berta stepped out from behind the women and aimed her spear gun. She was scared, but her hand was steady, she'd done this all before.

"Get outta my way, Tatiana!" she shouted just before pulling the trigger. Tatiana ducked as she swung her crowbar, busting the kneecaps of Walter in the process. Walter dropped to the ground. Berta had been aiming for Rosalyn's undead husband, but instead killed another white coat behind him. One yank of her spear and the sickening crunch of breaking skull assaulted their ears.

Yet, it was still better than the sound of Rosalyn's keening. Tatiana jumped up again and swung her crowbar once more. The comforting thunk of metal against bone resulted. The splat of old gloopy brains against the nearest wall followed.

This was fun, Tatiana decided.

The count was currently two down, one injured, but the number was climbing. Pippa's shaking hand settled and she got lost in the excitement of the kill. She stepped out, away from her friends and came face to face with a woman in a lab coat. Her brown hair, once long and straight and caught to one side with a hair clip, was now tangled and bloody. Pippa pulled her arm up quickly and bought it to the forehead of the woman, then pulled the trigger. She was not prepared for the recoil. It shot up her arm and she actually dropped the gun. Jumping back, she checked to see if the lab woman was dead.

Three down.

She ducked down and grabbed the gun. As she stood, she looked around. Tatiana had killed another zombie and Berta had killed two more.

That just left five zombies. This was so doable, Pippa decided as she rubbed the squirmy little child in her belly.

***

"Walter." Her voice was feeble now as she crawled across the dusty hall towards the man she married as soon as she'd turned eighteen. His marbled eyes heard her voice; his head lifting once more, mouth open, catching the scent of her.

He still remembers me.

"Walter, baby."

He moaned in response and started dragging himself towards her. Dark, thick blood oozed out of his shattered kneecaps but there was no pain etched on his face.

Rosalyn reached out and held his hand. It was cold and rough, dead skin chapped and ragged from tasks that Rosalyn didn't dare think about.

"I love you baby," she said quietly, tears trickling down her cheeks.

Walter moaned in agreement and then ripped out her throat.

***

Pippa saw the whole thing. Her feet moved, yet not quickly enough. Her hand was raised but she was not a good shot, so never even had a chance to pull the trigger.

"NOOOOOOOO!"

Tatiana turned and saw her newly found friend lying in a puddle of her own ooze. Warm blood still shot out of her severed artery. Walter drank it like it was the elixir of youth.

Berta, who was the closest, was horrified by what she saw. It still didn't stop her from plunging her fully loaded spear gun into the head of Walter though. He slumped next to his wife.

"How long before she reanimates?" Berta asked.

But there was no time for a reply. Four more of the undead had to be dealt with.

113

And these four meant business. They huddled together, shuffling, hands outstretched. The three women also pulled themselves together, unsure of how to approach them.

Berta pulled her spear gun free from Walter, thankful that she didn't have to reload. She cocked the gun and shot.

It was the first time that day she's missed her target.

The zombie she hit yowled in frustration as the spear hit him in his shoulder. One arm automatically dropped as its severed nerve gave way. She threw her weapon to the ground, not risking pulling the live zombie closer to her in order to wrestle her spear free.

Tatiana swung her crowbar and also missed.

The group separated, Tatiana went to the left, Berta to the right. Pippa hugged her gun and shook in fright. The group of zombies howled in excitement and lunged at Pippa, she jumped back, tripped over Rosalyn's outstretched arm, and fell on her behind. The zombies flew into a frenzy.

Well, two of them did. Berta and Tatiana had disposed of the others.

"Wesley!" Pippa shouted as she cowered on the ground.

"Pippa!" was the returning scream.

"Shoot Pippa!" Tatiana called.

This was possibly the dumbest suggestion she could have given.

Five shots popped off in rapid succession. Not one of them hit their target. Two whizzed close to Berta's face though.

"Stop it, Pippa!" she'd shouted, but the gun was empty before she'd finished her sentence.

And still the zombie's descended.

Berta raced forward and pushed the two zombies. They toppled over like a pair of macabre dominos. Tatiana took advantage of their confusion and swung her trusty crowbar. The force behind it was so strong it took the zombie's head clear off its shoulders. If their lives didn't depend on their quick reflexes, the group would have laughed at the sight of the head as it rolled down the hall, bouncing off a wall and then coming to a stop at the door to the elevator.

The last zombie panicked. This surprised Tatiana, since she thought they had no other emotion than 'feed me'. And then she remembered Peter. He'd remembered her.

This chicken shit zombie must still have a thought or two left rattling around in his empty head, she thought as she sprinted after the retreating figure. Before she had a chance to swing her crowbar, Berta fired her spear gun and ended the war.

The silence was golden as they stood around and grinned. They'd done it!

"Hello?" It was a feeble whisper that caught in Wesley's throat as he spoke.

"Wesley!" Pippa was up and off that floor as quick as a pregnant woman can be. She staggered across the hallway and into the room that held her boyfriend.

***

It had taken longer to find the key and free Wesley from his cell than it had taken the women to kill all the zombies.

None of them had been game to shoot Rosalyn in the head either, so Tatiana had dragged her body into another room and shut the door. She hoped Rosalyn didn't reanimate like Peter or the chicken shit zombie had, with thoughts still in her head. But when they left the forensic unit, there still wasn't a peep from that room, so they didn't have a chance to find out.

Each woman had to live with the guilt of that.

Wesley explained what had happened to him while they drove home. Berta cried and didn't listen. Tatiana tried to listen, though she was still too numb to comprehend his words. Pippa was the only one who paid him any attention. She held his hand and stared at him with adoration as his story unfolded.

And Rosalyn was lucky she wasn't there to hear it - since it was Walter who had originally locked Wesley up.

He'd discovered Wesley's journal and the fact that he had withheld the possible cure from everyone. Walter thought he was doing the right thing, or so he kept telling Wesley. The whole time though, Walter took blood samples and manipulated Wesley's immunity. The cure had been discovered, but not before Walter had been bitten by the chicken shit zombie.

Pippa should have made them turn back then to retrieve the notes and vials of unused vaccine against the undead.

Instead she continued to stroke her boyfriend's hand and rest her head on his shoulder.

That night they three women cried and cried. Rosalyn's death shook them up more than they realised. Berta clung to her cat, ignoring the wheezes and snuffles as she stroked him. Tatiana raided the surrounding houses and found enough booze and cigarettes to keep her happy.

Pippa cried, but she was also thankful for the return of Wesley. It was their joyful reunion and early resulting early retirement to their room that kept Pippa safe. Wesley, of course, was immune.

***

Tatiana had finished the entire bottle of whiskey. Everything was now funny as well as being viewed in double vision.

So the sight of Martin jumping from Berta's lap and digging his fangs into the throat of his owner was at first something for her to giggle about. She pointed and laughed some more before she felt the warm, wet spray of Berta's blood against her cheek.

Her giggling stopped as she wiped her hand across her face. Looking at the red on her fingers confused her, so she raised her eyes once more to Berta.

All she saw were the marble eyes of Berta's cat and then the pain as he tore into her face.

Diary of Pippa Roscoe to her unborn child February 23rd
(73 days after the first reported outbreak)
Little One, We have reached the farm that the four of us first set out to find:
Berta, Tatiana, Rosalyn and I.
They didn't make it. But, instead, you have your daddy back!
It's so peaceful up here. The house we picked isn't actually a farm, but it is set high on the side of a hill, so we can see danger coming. There is only one road in, which sometimes worries me, but at least there are now a bunch of paths tracked through the trees, so we have plenty of escape routes if need be.
Life is quiet, peaceful, restful, sad.
I wonder if you will be immune like your dad.
I think that you are.
I think that is what is keeping me alive.
Love always,
Mamma Pippa.

The End.

117

*That was the concluding part of Zombie Apocalypse Now!
Feel free to visit me at <u>racheltsoumbakos.wordpress.com</u> and tell me what
you thought of the ending.*

Dark Verse

Physician: Dr. Salam
7128-DV758JJ

Joseph Patchem
Omar ZahZah

Murmurs and wisps of words . . . It's always the same, each night. Little rumbles and small noises flood me with the stench of sin.

Over and over, they call to me with rancor and hate, slurring speech through dead eyes, dried throats and seeping wounds
until they manifest
clacking their skeletal teeth:
"Kill! Kill! Kill!"

Suicide is my only option.

I've thought about it
very carefully:
I don't want a wife
I don't want kids
I don't want money
I don't want to grow up
I don't want a house
I want you
to take me to a clearing
and hack off my arms and legs with an axe
and let me bleed out
and pick out my ribs
and build a little house
for the birds passing by.
And bring this with you
and rip it to bits
to line
The inside.
Only wait
a little bit
for the first bird to come.
You won't understand
the sounds he'll make.
He'll be saying
Goodbye.

On the
Record

We are pleased to introduce horror writer Brian Moreland. He is the author of titles including *Dead of Winter*, *The Girl from the Blood Coven*, *The Witching House* and *Shadows in the Mist*, which won a gold medal at the 2007 Independent Publishers Awards for best horror novel.

What was your first experience of the horror genre?

Brian Moreland: I started watching horror movies at a very young age. My mom and I used to watch double-creature features every Saturday on TV. From that experience, I associated being scared with having fun. I was also into reading comic books and seemed to gravitate toward the comics where a super hero was battling some kind of monster. When I got into my teens, I discovered Stephen King's short story collections and that's when I learned that reading horror can be even more fun than watching it on TV or at the movies.

While you were growing up did you have a favourite genre of horror that you would always gravitate to?

BM: I loved monsters in general, especially vampires, werewolves, aliens and just about anything with fangs and claws. The original *The Howling* movie is one of my all-time favourites. Other movies that I loved were *The Thing*, *Prophecy*, *Humanoids from the Deep*, *Day of the Triffids* and *Alien*. I used to read magazines like *Famous Monsters in Filmland* and *Fangoria*. I collected dozens of monster toys too.

When you started writing back in college, did you send any of your work out to agents or publishers?

BM: Yes, I wrote my first novel at age 19. It was only 113 pages and today would be considered a novella. But back then agents and publishers were only looking for novels. I submitted to a variety of agents and got several rejection letters. One agent was so impressed with my talent at such a young age that he called me and offered some personal advice. He said that my writing was really good and showed promise. He recommended that I take some writing classes and flesh out my story to about 100,000 words and contact him again in a couple years. At the time, it was hard to hear that I still had a lot of learning to do before I would see my book in print, but that agent's advice encouraged me to keep writing and learning.

Do you ever look back over the pieces you wrote in college and think about re-writing them?

BM: Yes, my first published novel, *Shadows in the Mist,* is an expanded version of a short screenplay that I wrote in a screenwriting class. The assignment was to write a 30-page script for our favourite TV show, so I wrote a supernatural WWII script called "The Refuge" as an episode of *Tales from the Crypt.* A couple years after college, I rewrote that script to be a short story, which later evolved into a full-length novel. It's ironic that at this year's Texas Frightmare Weekend convention in Dallas I got to do a book signing with the Crypt Keeper.

More recently, I've updated my very first novel - the one I wrote in college at age 19. It was originally titled *Skinners,* but that title has already been used, so I changed it to *The Devil's Woods.* Some of the characters in that novel have been with me for over 25 years. It was fun revisiting the story that got me into writing, but it was also a lot of work because my writing style has changed so much. I kept the basic story line, but had to completely re-write all the prose and dialogue. I also added several new characters and over a dozen new scenes. *The Devil's Woods* releases through Samhain Horror December 2nd, 2013. Here is the synopsis:

Fear wears many skins. Deep within the Canadian wilderness, people have been disappearing for over a century. There is a place the locals call "the Devil's Woods," but to speak of it will only bring the devil to your door. It is a place so evil that even animals avoid it.

When their father's expedition team goes missing, Kyle Elkheart and his brother and sister return to the abandoned Cree Indian reservation where they were born. Kyle can see ghosts that haunt the woods surrounding the village—and they seem to be trying to warn him. The search for their father will lead Kyle and his siblings to the dark heart of the legendary forest, where their mission will quickly become a fight for survival.

It's well documented that rejection is part of the writing process. If you do get a rejection letter, how do you process it before moving on?

BM: When I was a young writer, getting rejection letters really stung my ego. I was so certain that I had written some good stories and all I needed was some agent or publisher to believe in me and give me a shot. I've learned to accept rejection and move on quickly. I see each rejection letter as a stepping stone on the path to connecting with the right agent or the right publisher. To me, it's not worth going into business with a person or company that isn't as passionate about your books as you are. Sometimes you're better off getting a "no" and crossing them off your list. I'm a big believer that if you keep pursuing something relentlessly, you'll eventually achieve success. It's tenacious persistence that has gotten me to where I am today.

BM: I don't really have a lot of pet peeves. I read for entertainment and am not really that critical of other works. A writer's story either hooks me or it doesn't. I have a short attention span, so for the most part I'll just move on to the next story.

You have recorded success in both the self-publishing and traditional publishing arenas. If you were starting out again now, would you hold out for a publisher or would you go self-published to get the ball rolling?

BM: I would follow a similar path: 1.) submit to agents first to see if I can land a big publishing contract 2.) after several months have passed, if I've accumulated rejection slips with no deal on the horizon, I would self-publish to get the ball rolling 3.) After getting my first book out and generating some book sales, I'd continue to pursue a book deal with a mid-to-large sized publisher.

The biggest difference between now and my first go-round, I'd probably self-publish much faster. A few years back it was frowned upon to self-publish and there weren't as many outlets for authors to do it themselves as there are now. The invention of ebooks
and Print-on-Demand printing has made it so much easier and inexpensive to self-publish.

You signed with Penguin / Putnam for Shadows in the Mist, but now you are signed with Samhain Publishing. Do you think it is better going with a genre specific publisher?

BM: Absolutely. I've had a much more enjoyable experience going with a mid-sized genre-specific publisher like Samhain Horror. They give me and my books more personal attention and market my books to the right audience. They ask for my input on cover design and even let me design 4 out of 5 of my covers, using my own artwork. I've also gotten to meet several established horror authors whose books are being published alongside mine. When I was at Penguin / Putnam, I never met any of their authors and I felt alone. With Samhain Horror, I feel like I'm part of a family. That goes for the entire Samhain Publishing staff, as well. They're good people.

Samhain Publishing is well respected within the convention circles and they are always present. You recently attended the HorrorHound weekend, how was that?

BM: An absolute blast. Samhain Horror was the main sponsor, so we had a nice large booth at the front. They supplied all the books, and all I had to do was show up for the three-day signing. I got to autograph books alongside fellow authors Kristopher Rufty, Jonathan Janz and David Searls. We were swarmed by horror fans and we sold out of our books. I love attending horror cons. This year's HorrorHound drew an enormous crowd thanks to the cast of *The Walking Dead* being there. I also got to tour Cincinnati, which is a beautiful city. Next to writing fiction, travelling to do book signings and meet horror fans is where the juice is for me.

Along with other writers, you have a great presence on Facebook and writing your blog "Dark Lucidity". You always seem to make time to answer your readers' questions. How important do you think social media is for a writer, and where do you draw the line regarding privacy?

BM: Thanks, it took me three years to build up that presence and now it's paying off. For little-known authors, social media is a necessity for readers discovering your books. There are so many books on the market that having product pages on Amazon and BarnesandNoble.com is not enough to generate book sales.

Facebook, Twitter and Goodreads are great places to connect directly with fans and to get feedback after someone has read something you've written. I love it when a reader sends me a FB email or writes on my wall or tweets about my book. It reminds me that people are, in fact, reading my books, and it's rewarding to see that my story has had a positive impact on someone else. Without social media, I would not have reached the number of readers that I'm reaching now.

As far as drawing the line regarding privacy, I'm a very private person. I post updates about my books and signings and have friendly discussions on social media. I cheer people on and share a funny picture or cartoon every now and then. I don't talk about religion or politics, debate with people, chastise critics or share personal information about my family. I like to keep the topics light and centered around my books, hobbies and career as a writer.

With so much writing that you do, how do you find the time? Do you have a set routine that you stick to?

BM: I make the time when I can. I work another career running my own business as a book editor/designer and film/video editor. When I get busy with client projects, I don't get a lot of writing done. I pretty much write in creative "sprints" when I'm in between projects. I like to go on 7-10 day writing sabbaticals and get into hyper-focus on a novel. I'll stay at a private cabin and do nothing but write for a long weekend or week. During my sabbaticals I can write 100 to 150 pages. Once I've written a first draft, I'll get up around 5:00 a.m. and work on my manuscript during the early morning hours before work.

You mention on your Bio that you are into film / video editing, do you ever think about making book trailers and how do you feel about them?

BM: I had thought about it when the concept of book trailers first came about. But after doing some research, I got the impression from other writers that book trailers don't necessarily lead to many viewings or book sales. My German publisher did create a trailer for *Shadows in the Mist,* which they titled *Schattenkrieger.* You can view the trailer at
http://www.youtube.com/watch?v=0LeCFq0bkgk

Can you tell us a little about the next book you have planned?

BM: Yes, this summer I'm thrilled to release two back-to-back stories about witches. First in July, people with e-readers can download my free short story *The Girl from the Blood Coven*. This terrifying short tale about a massacre at a hippy commune in 1972 sets up the mystery for my novella *The Witching House*, which releases August 6th. Here's a synopsis for each ebook:

The Girl from the Blood Coven

Who—or what—killed them all? In this short story prelude to *The Witching House*, the year is 1972. Sheriff Travis Keagan is enjoying a beer at the local roadhouse when a blood-soaked girl enters the bar. Terrified and trembling, Abigail Blackwood claims her entire family was massacred at the nearby hippy commune in the woods. But when Sheriff Keagan and his deputies investigate the Blevins House, they discover there's more to Abigail's story than she's told them. Much more.

The Witching House

Some houses should be left alone. In 1972, twenty-five people were brutally murdered in one of the bloodiest massacres in Texas history. The mystery of who committed the killings remains unsolved.

Forty years later, Sarah Donovan is dating an exciting man, Dean Stratton. Sarah's scared of just about everything—heights, tight places, the dark—but today she must confront all her fears, as she joins Dean and another couple on an exploring adventure. The old abandoned Blevins House, the scene of the gruesome massacre, is rumored to be haunted. The two couples are about to discover the

mysterious house has been waiting all these years, craving fresh prey. And down in the cellar they will encounter a monstrous creature that hungers for more than just human flesh.

What was the best piece of advice you ever received about writing?

BM: Back when I was taking a workshop in Rome, Italy with bestselling horror author John Saul, I was still struggling to finish my novel *Shadows in the Mist*. When John asked what was keeping me from finishing the book, I gave him a whole bunch of excuses. John told me straight up, "Just finish the *damn* book."

A few months later, I was at the Maui Writer's Conference in Hawaii, shopping my unfinished manuscript to agents and editors, when I ran into John Saul again. He asked me how the book was going, and I humbly told him it was still half-finished. When he asked why, I gave him some more lame excuses about life events keeping me from having the time to focus on finishing.

John Saul challenged me to stop making excuses. When he autographed his latest bestselling horror novel for me, he wrote "Just finish the *damn* book." I looked up to John Saul, because he was one of my favourite writers and has published over a dozen bestselling novels. I realized right then and there if I wanted to be a successful author with multiple books published, I had to stop making excuses and keep writing until I reached the end of my books. Once I stopped giving in to excuses, I began to see my books go from half-finished manuscripts to books selling worldwide.

Finally before we let you go. Do you have a piece of advice for our readers who are looking to improve their writing?

BM: Yes, keep learning about the craft of writing. Keep honing your craft. Even though I've published several books now, I still read books on how to write a better story, plot, dialogue, etc. I study horror writers, as well as other genres, like romance, mystery, science fiction, YA, comedy and the classics. I want my writing to continue to evolve and be fresh, so I'm always challenging myself to push the boundaries of my writing. I recommend every writer push themselves to write new material that takes their writing into new directions.

For writers seeking to be published, here's an additional piece of advice I'd give about signing on with a small or mid-sized publisher: If a publisher shows interest in you, before signing a contract, go look at their website and see what kinds of titles they are publishing. Have they published several books in your genre or just one or two? Do you love the cover designs or are they crappy clip-art designs that looked like they were done by a 5th grader?

If a publisher is not going to design a high-quality book for you, it won't sell and will get lost in a sea of poorly published books.

Go to your nearest Barnes and Noble or favourite book store and see if they can order any of this publisher's titles. If their books aren't available to book stores neither will your book be. Lastly, Google the publisher's name and see if they have a web presence and are advertising on other websites. If they aren't at least marketing their line of books, then the most they can offer you is editing, book design and posting your book on Amazon, which doesn't equate to sales unless you, yourself, send people to that page. If that's the case, you might as well self-publish and keep a larger percentage of the profit.

Thank you very much for spending time with us, Brian, we hope the next book is a hit and we look forward to seeing what you and Samhain Publishing has in store for the horror genre.

BM: Thanks so much for having me here on *Sanitarium*. It's been an honor.

About Brian MoreLand:

Brian Moreland writes novels and short stories of horror and supernatural suspense. His books include *Dead of Winter*, *Shadows in the Mist*, *The Girl from the Blood Coven*, *The Witching House*, and *The Devil's Woods*. Brian lives in Dallas, Texas where he is diligently writing his next horror novel. You can join his mailing list at http:// www.brianmoreland.com/

Twitter: @BrianMoreland

Like Brian's Facebook page: http://www.facebook.com/ HorrorAuthorBrianMoreland

Brian's blog: http://www.brianmoreland.blogspot.com

"Where The Horror Happens" with Angeline Trevena

We catch up with Angeline to talk horror and about her work ethic.

So what is your workspace like?

Generally an absolute mess.

And I can't work in mess, so every time I sit down to write I have to spend ten minutes tidying up first. I still hope that one day I'll learn to keep the area tidy all the time! It's not very horror-esque, with my bright pink desk, and sitting right next to a window does mean that I end up doing a lot of curtain-twitching when I should be writing! But it's my little space, and that's what matters.

Do you have a go-to gadget / app or service that you cannot live without?

I'm quite behind everyone else with technology; I don't own a smartphone, iPad or e-reader. I've simply not yet found the need for them. But I do have a few go-to websites that I couldn't live without. Name generators Seventh Sanctum and Cult of Squid are two of my most visited sites, as well as Horror Tree where I go to find my next submissions call.

Do you have a set routine while you work?

Routine is something that had to go out of the window when I had my son eight months ago. My whole life revolves around feed times and nap times; something my muse has refused to co-ordinate with. Most of my writing is done in short snatches of time. If I'm really up against a deadline, the internet and the TV get turned off, and the Chronicles of Narnia soundtrack gets turned on. That's when people know I'm serious, so they tend to stay out of the way!

What is the best piece of advice you have ever received?

It was more of a comment than a piece of advice, but I recall it every time I lose my nerve. I studied Drama and Writing at university, and one of our tutors asked us to write a piece about ourselves and our future careers. I wrote that I couldn't imagine writing ever being anything more than just a hobby. My tutor's comment simply said 'That would be a shame'. That was the first time I realised that perhaps a writing career really was possible.

Do you have a final piece of advice for our readers?

Write what you love. I see so many writers chasing the trends, and stressing out trying to predict what the next popular genre will be. I strongly believe that you write best when you're excited about your project. If you're excited about it, your enthusiasm will come through in your words, and your readers will be excited about it too. You're unlikely to make your fortune through writing, so enjoy it, don't turn it into a chore.

About Angeline:

Angeline Trevena is a horror and fantasy writer living above a milkshake shop in the south west of England. The unlikeliest of horror writers, Angeline is scared of the dark and refuses to say Candyman's name five times.

She has short stories published by Angelic Knight Press, Crooked Cat Publishing, and Mirador Publishing, with stories published by Horrified Press and

Fringeworks due out later this year. She also writes a monthly column for Horror Tree and is an active blogger.

Angeline is supposed to be working on her first novel, if only she can pull herself away from short stories for a while. You can find out more by visiting her website at

http://angelinetrevena.co.uk/

If you have any feedback or would like to leave a review please
head over to Amazon and share your thoughts about Sanitarium.

Thank you for your time and we salute your
love for all things horror.